THE

HUMAN

CONDITION

Anthology

Edited by MJ Moores

Infinite Pathways
PRESS

CANADA

The Human Condition Anthology

Copyright © Infinite Pathways Press, 2016

Published in Canada by
Infinite Pathways Press
P.O. Box 4
Caledon Village, Ontario
L7K 3L3

ISBN 978-1-988044-05-7

For permission to use material from the product, submit a request online at www.infinite-pathways.org

Every effort has been made to trace ownership of all copyrighted material and to secure permission from copyright holders.

PREFACE

to THE HUMAN CONDITION ANTHOLOGY

From day one, the goal of Infinite Pathways Press has been to provide a stable editing and publicity resource for new and emerging authors around the globe. We offer free platform building services from article contribution, to editing & publicity tips, excerpts of fiction, creative non-fiction, and memoir, to book reviews and book & author spotlights.

One of our early mandates focused on providing an opportunity for Canadian authors to participate in writing competitions with their peers. This anthology not only celebrates the winners and honourable mentions in these contests—short story, flash fiction, and poetry—but extends itself one step further to encompass work from 2015's open submissions for writers and poets of all genres.

The Human Condition Anthology is a reflection of humanity's trials, tribulations, wants, needs, and desires as they span from seasons, to decades, years, hours, and the minutia of time. Each piece provides a glimpse into what it means to be human—flawed, glorious, and everything in between.

MJ Moores, Editor

INTRODUCTION

by Isobel Warren – *Author, Journalist, Teacher, & Publisher*

Plus ça change, plus c'est la même chose.

Thankfully for those who love books and writing, "la même chose" in this case is the art and craft of writing – that curious drive to explore and recount life's joys and tragedies, triumphs and fears, loves and losses via the warp and weft of words.

As bookstores close, book sections shrink, writers' incomes shrivel, TV channels enchant, and aspiring writers are urged to take up fast food service or basket weaving to support their unfortunate addiction, rumours of our imminent demise run rampant. But writing continues to live and even to flourish. The written word may manifest itself via a different medium or tool, but the fact remains that thanks to courageous publishers and adamant scribes, many, many people continue to stick their noses into a book or a tablet and read. Plus ça change, plus c'est la même chose.

And so The Human Condition emerges as a valuable platform for Canadian writers (who are myriad but mostly hidden).

With its varied menu of poetry, flash fiction, and longer narratives, ranging boldly through life's glories and vicissitudes, telling very human stories that inspire and enrich, The Human Condition, is thus well named and an engrossing read. These 23 writers, skilled and perceptive, reflect the realities of today and the future of Canadian publishing.

The Human Condition is also a testament to the courage of its editor and publisher, MJ Moores, who poured all of her considerable experience and energies into assembling this fine anthology and creating a book with both literary merit and eye appeal.

I salute and honour all of you. May your words take flight to delight a world of readers and prove once again that the pleasures of writing and reading are la même chose.

Isobel Warren
Newmarket, Ontario

Isobel Warren's writing career has spanned more than five decades, from newspaper journalism to TV, magazine publishing to book publishing, travel writing to fiction writing plus decades of teaching and mentoring entry level writers at U of T, Ryerson, Seneca and lately, Newmarket Public Library. Her most recent book is *In Them Days*, a fictional view of a remote Canadian farming community a century ago. She founded Hands, The Canadian Craft Magazine, published it throughout the eighties and retains a keen interest in crafts. She lives, writes and quilts in Newmarket with two spoiled cats and her partner in life and work, Milan Chvostek, award winning former producer of CBC-TV's The Nature of Things.

CONTENTS

Anthology

FLASH FICTION

SHORT STORIES

soul

subtle *love* awakening

ephemeral?

seductive emotive

POETRY

truth *sensual* ephemeral
lies
experience enticing *quiet torment*
rejoice
hate

visceral

awaken

Raw

Erika Willaert

Skin on skin

Breath meets breast

Mouth is craving

Tonguing, tracing

Lips aquiver

Sending shivers

Pressure mounting

Pulse rebounding

Tasting pleasure

Touching together

Fingers lacing

Heartbeat racing

Senseless

Still

Sigh

1st Place Winner: Infinite Pathways Poetry Competition

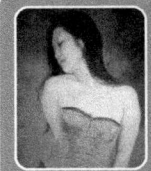

Dancer by training and a teacher by trade, Erika Willaert is usually out in the forest with her two dogs or attending a live performance or movie where she is often the loudest audience member, much to the dismay of her children.

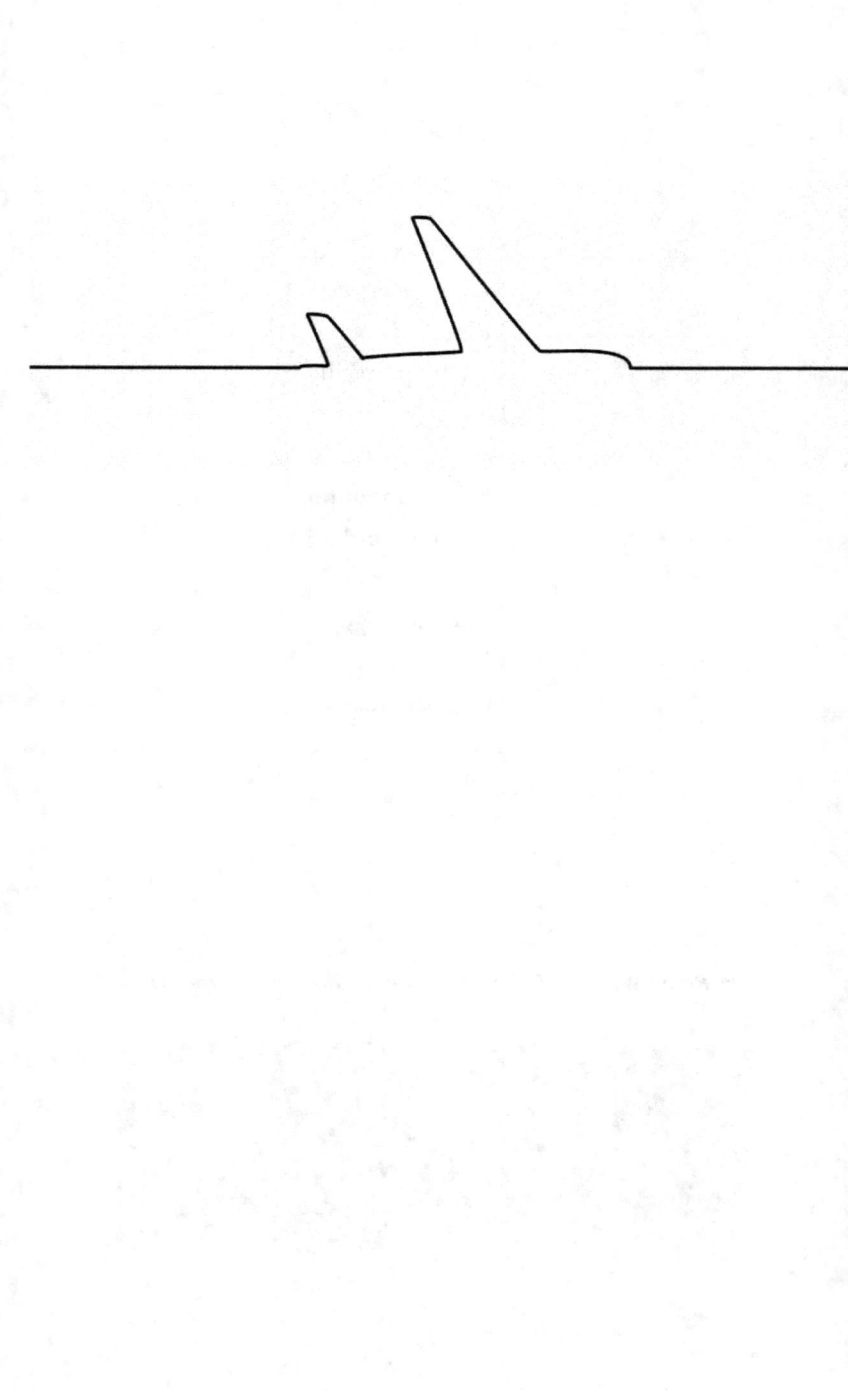

Flight Over Bay of Bengal

A Gathering Storm
Colleen Engelhardt

The fog lays thick and heavy, like the damp humidity of
the jungle,
a mirror image of the dense, oppressive night sky.
Unbeknownst to those on the ground
(the fog obscuring any view),
a battle rages on with the sky high above.

By day, the cumulo-nimbus clouds, like ethereal beings,
rose 30,000 to 40,000 feet.
By night, they became towering giants
whose awesome grasp, one could only hope to escape.

"Clouds, tall like the majestic Kauri Pine, forced us low
that night."
(reports the navigator)
"Flying was clear just below the clouds,
but dangerous, being so low.
All's well, till, like the sudden onslaught of a monsoon,
we shot upwards, uncontrollably."

"Rooted to floor, like the ancient roots of the baobab
we shot continually upwards.

Power cut, nose hard down but to no avail.
Just as suddenly,
we began to fall."

Nature, like a tiger playing with a mouse, tossed metal
and man.
Hope faded as hunter became prey.
Hurtling, plummeting
STOP
Nose pulled up -- disaster averted.

"We had dropped to about 500 feet,
(reports the navigator)
sending us off course.
Course reset we flew off,
failing to understand our danger,
like Icarus as he approached the sun."

Passengers, strapped in seats, stomachs in throats,
hand rests gripped – recovery is not so easily achieved.
A definitive experience?
Reality re-imposes; it's just another defiance of death.

And below, people yawn in a sleepy, sloth-like village,
unaware of the fog, the clouds, of the tumultuous
warring sky.

They sleep on, a mirror of their homes' attitudes,
never realizing the men of the skies
are Hercules in disguise.

2nd Place Winner: Infinite Pathways Poetry Competition

A writer from an early age, Colleen began to pursue this interest more seriously following her university degrees. Colleen's own passion for writing has led to her desire to share it with others in both her personal and professional fields.

The Storm

Joanna Gale

Thunder raps gently at the front door. Dark clouds
come and go. Inside the eerie stillness, I want to hear
this storm as I prepare soup, and set up the ironing.
Thought I could get away without these distractions —
Straight forward, stuff of women's work; the tatting
stitched together with the plain in fine fashion,
like some poems I enjoy. *Different sensibilities —*
the desires of men, the desires of women? Slowly, I peel
the layers of onion, chop celery and slice mushroom
sautéed for chicken broth. A sudden downpour
drenches the outside drought. Mud puddles pool.
For a moment, power is lost, and our radio skips
a beat. The colour of air, a musky green, drowns
the earth tone trees holding steady in this torrential
soak. Thunder booms like huge bowling balls rumbling
across overhead lane ways. Rain pounds pavement,
bounces teardrop reflections. *Storms, such brutal beasts,*
blast in with their violent force and yet, can bring a sense
of cleansing, clarity, relief. And, where is my husband?
One last roll of thunder falls a gentler rain. Roads
glisten along with all the green leafy sheens —
after-image flashes like those a camera imprints
on the frontal lobes of our brain. *This collar*
needs smoothing. I re-steam and rework the heavy

creases out — *(not perfect, not bad). How did I miss these areas on flat pieces of linen and lace?* Dark clouds come and go. A drip   drop splats the clay pots outside my patio window. *Needed this correction.* The radio bleeps.

3rd Place Winner: Infinite Pathways Poetry Competition

Joanna Gale has been published in newsletters, chapbooks, anthologies, magazines and other periodicals, as well as on-line. She is a retired Registered Nurse, who currently lives in Markham, Ontario, with her husband, not too far from her son and his family.

And You'll Whisper

Amanda Walke

Its not it's words or it's wishes
Its it's purpose and how it hurts us.

The undoing comes from them
comes to us, looking, sounding like a wren,
calls to us, just like the kinglet himself.
But searching for something specific,
something inside of you, so they take from you,
they slice that, which feeds them, from you,
to feast, to fill an appetite you grew,
but wanted nothing of, and never knew.

Until you turned away, turned around,
turned from them, and you were found.
To be undressed of what you kept unguarded with gold,
an out of sight, an untouchable.

Now to be touched by them, had by them,
without so much as touching you, unless be it pretend.
You thief! You've taken bits, bought from me not sold,
rich off and out of ways not recognized by those unless the soul.

So see yourself with pockets full of me.
Trade with others, that which not a mirror can see,
will not reflect, that which you did,
you do, you'll die before you see,

with only hopes it makes your insides
feel like you've been outside far too long at sea.

So tell your troop of trailsmen,
let it speak from you wholly, if you can.
But your words won't be heard by me, the whisper …

You can't   whisper   undoings   through untrimmed trees
with   out   catch   ing   fire   from me.

Infinite Pathways' Poetry Contest Judge

Amanda Walke is passionate about poetry, teaching, and travelling. What Amanda took away from university is that the poet is an artist and arborist of words. The best poetry comes from a seed of thought or feeling from somewhere deep within, and sprouts out wildly, unruly and unrelentingly.

Turn Left

Sheila Horne

You are the man you
chose to be. Not what I hoped
or planned when you were small
and I promised not to drive
down the street. Not to stop
for the light. Not to turn left
but stay, and cuddle you forever.
Now, from my window I watch you
walk out of the house. Drive
down the street. Stop for the light
and turn left into your life.

Dedicated to Adam

Sheila Horne's articles, poems and short stories
have been published in various magazines and
anthologies. She facilitates writing programs and
is a member of The Markham Village Writers and
The Writers' Community of York Region.

watching women

Gary Johnson

Laying in the long grass
out of my comfortable lair
a spent force
no longer in the hunt
eunuched by age
defanged and roarless
respected but no threat
just an old male animal
growling from the side lines
unseen on a mall bench

A graduate from Ryerson's Radio & Television, Gary was employed at CBC before striking out on his own. Currently, he works for Ontario Farm Fresh growing garlic and cut flowers along with his wife Cathy.

Facing the Inevitable

S. B. Barak

I'm glad we don't believe in open caskets —
although at that point it's definitely someone else's
job to make you look good.

Would they hide the greys? try to smooth off all
the callouses on your fingertips? —
thinking that just one look at your babyface,

long hair, and earring stud
would suffice to say
"cool, he was a musician!" —

that cultivated rocker image
 à la Paul McCartney — the cute, fun one —
with the big brown eyes that amplified

my faults under a magnifying glass until I became
a walking distortion that even my guardian angel
might not right away recognize.

It complicates things forever
once you have kids together; jarring
everyday and only-once renditions of felicity

and stacked cords of sorrow.
When you are gone, how will I be able to forget
enough to comfort them?

Anthology

Mother of four and musician, S. B. Barak harmonizes her writerly interests exploring poetic inquiry as a research method, in her doctoral work in Critical Disability Studies.

Isn't ...

Harry Posner

I just can't do it anymore
I just can't do it anymore
because the feeling isn't there
I just can't do it anymore

because the feeling isn't there
I can't lift a finger
I can't lift a finger
because the feeling isn't there

just isn't there
wasn't never will
because the feeling isn't there
I just can't do it anymore anymore

because it's not about love
and it's not about doors
it's not about age
or bones or deleted files
because it's not about love
I just can't do it anymore
I can't lift a finger
because the feeling isn't there

because it's not about love
doors
bones

The Human Condition

files
fingers
emptiness emptiness emptiness
echoes down a long hall
loss
regret
stagnation
doing or not doing
having or not having
because the feeling isn't there
I can't lift a file
finger bones
regret doors
I just can't do it anymore

having or not having
lost bones or found fingers
empty promises promises promises
scrubbed rooms files
abrupt leavings
tender wounds
I just can't do it anymore
I can't lift a finger
because the feeling isn't there

help or salve or fix
broken bones
unhinged doors
stagnant regret
runaway words

I can't lift a finger tongue
I just can't do it anymore
because the feeling isn't there
it isn't there it isn't there
it just isn't there isn't there
it just isn't isn't isn't

A member of Words Aloud poetry collective, the Headwaters Writers Guild, Writers Ink Alton, and Associate Member of the League of Canadian Poets, **Harry Posner** has published books of poetry--*Wordbirds*; novels--*Charivari* and *A Softness in the Eyes*; flash fiction--*Little Exits*; and a CD of audio poetry--*In The Event of True Happiness*.   **www.posnerbooks.com**

without covers

Carol Thomson

superb feats of engineering
different configurations
amazing old or new
each precious to its owner
enhanced by art
embellished by ink
physically fit or not
each one absolutely unique
bathed in sunshine
dark to light in colour
sometimes carved
by a surgeon's knife
evolved by nature
perfumed and powdered
beautiful beyond words
our bodies
with no tan lines

Carol Thomson is an award-winning poet for adults and children alike. As an educator she inspires children to develop their writing and speaking skills. Carol illustrates the picture books she creates for children and has won awards for her artwork.

Unite Glimpse

Empathize Powerful Fiction

Shot Reveal

Peek Vignette Snap

FLASHFICTION Believe

Feel Moment

Emotion Learn

Imagine

Understand

Talking to Teddy Under the Covers
By Cheryl MacLean

Mommy smelled like powder.

No, not the white powder she rubs on me after my bath, the pink powder she puts on her face with the big soft brush that she tickles my nose with and makes me sneeze.

She smelled like that.

Daddy didn't tell me not to wake her up today. He let me hold her hand and didn't say *shhh*. Usually when she's sleeping and I sneak in to lie down beside her, her hands are cold and I breathe on them to warm them up, like she does to me when I come in from making angels in the snow. But today they weren't cold like that. Her hand felt like my doll—smooth and plasticky—not like Mommy's hands at all.

Then Grandma pulled me away by my arm. She whispered something to Daddy that I couldn't hear and we all went out to Grandpa's big black car. Daddy sat in the front seat and wouldn't let me sit on his lap so I sat with Grandma in the back seat, but I pushed myself up against the door because she smelled like the attic in their old house on the farm, and she held my hand too tight.

Grandpa started backing up and I said, *Wait! What about Mommy?*

Daddy said she wasn't coming home.

Grandma put her bent up wrinkled hand on my cheek. It smelled like Mommy's ash tray on the back deck that fills up with rainwater and looks like cigarette soup—black at the bottom, brown in the middle, and puffed up cotton balls and orange pieces of paper floating on top like the alphabet noodles in my vegetable soup.

I begged Daddy to go back in and kiss her, like Sleeping Beauty, to wake her up so she could come home with us. But Daddy just puffed one of Mommy's cigarettes and Grandpa drove us home.

1st Place Winner: Infinite Pathways Flash Fiction

Cheryl MacLean has been a professional writer since before the turn of the century. After a short stint in the hard-edged world of journalism, she turned away from the bylined writing path to the anonymous world of technical writing, where she has published thousands of pages of scarce-read enterprise software documentation. Several years ago, with her forties growing ever larger on the horizon, Cheryl dusted off the right side of her brain and rekindled her dreams of writing creatively for pleasure. She is currently navigating the stormy waters of the publishing world with her first novel, has three other novels in progress, and is dabbling in short fiction, creative nonfiction and poetry.

Follow Cheryl on Twitter: @Writer_Cheryl

The Open Heart

By Elizabeth Girard

H is face looked awful: yellowish and swollen, pulled out of shape by the breathing tube taped to one side of his mouth. The machine it was attached to sucked and sighed, raising and lowering his chest.

That tape will leave marks on his skin, I thought.

I ached to touch him, to make him familiar and mine again but he belonged to the hospital now, to all these people who'd saved his life. The ICU nurse came in and I checked her face to see if she was kind. She looked tired.

"He'll be waking up soon," she said. "We wake them quickly. Then I'll remove the tube."

"I'd like to stay," I said.

"Can you take it?" She looked doubtful.

I nodded. I'd promised. This part frightened him more than the surgery.

"We can repair your husband's heart but his lungs are compromised," the surgeon had said. He looked down at his shoes. "We'll prepare for all eventualities."

A man wearing green scrubs brushed through the bedside curtains, one hand holding aloft a syringe filled with a clear liquid. He slid a shy smile my way but didn't speak.

"The anesthesiologist," explained the nurse.

He lifted an IV tube and injected the drug that would bring Peter out of his eight-hour sleep, then left. The nurse and I waited.

Within seconds Peter gave a great start and his eyes flew open, full of terror. Never had I seen an expression like that. Did his body remember what had been done to it when his mind wasn't looking? I picked up his limp hand.

"Pete? The surgery's over and the breathing tube's going to come out now. Don't be frightened, I'm here."

"He has to be able to follow my instructions," said the nurse. She turned to Peter. "Can you hear me?"

Her voice was loud.

I watched Peter struggle to obey her commands to lift a finger, wiggle his toes. He always tried so hard. Why had it taken me so long to see that? Pain squeezed my heart.

The tape left red marks.

"Open your mouth now, wide, wider. Good."

With a deft twist and a tug, the nurse had the breathing tube out, its ribbed surface slick. Peter coughed and took a raspy breath; I held mine and willed him to take another. He did, then a few more, and stopped.

"Peter?" said the nurse.

His eyelids were sliding shut.

A flame of anguish engulfed me, so searing I feared a stroke. God no. Please. No!

The nurse's movements were practiced, efficient; she didn't look tired anymore. Oxygen hissed, a mask appeared over Peter's face, another drug was injected. I waited.

At last the hush of his breathing resumed, tentative at first, then easier. I clung to his hand, my life. His eyes opened, calmer now, and found mine. Damn tears! Quick. Find a smile.

"Hello you," I said. "Welcome back."

2nd *Place Winner: Infinite Pathways Flash Fiction*

Elizabeth's first inspiration for writing was the novel, Gone With The Wind. She was a teenager, and heartsick at the thought that Scarlet should lose Rhett so she rewrote the ending. Several years later a colleague encouraged her to write poetry. She wrote short stories for her students throughout her career as an elementary teacher and after retirement, resumed writing poetry and began to write prose. She is currently working on her first novel. To her very great delight, Elizabeth's advancing years have brought an unexpected romance into her life, a blissful marriage between her love of learning and her love of the written word. Good thing her husband isn't the jealous type.

Absence

By Erika Willaert

For a moment, a stillness hung in the air, heavy yet hollow. Rose watched the balloon drift higher and farther than her eyes could reach. When it disappeared among the clouds, she turned away, her neck aching from the strain of her gaze.

There were no witnesses, only leftover streamers and empty wrappers strewn about the trampled grass. She picked her way toward the last remaining tent, its wide mouth billowing in the sudden gust of wind. Ducking inside, Rose tried not to look in the corner once occupied by a certain silk screen. The Great Mancini never graced the stage for more than three nights in one town, yet she missed him fiercely, despite his brief appearance.

Standing in the entrance, her slight silhouette glowing in the dying light of dusk, she heard a familiar rumble grow louder. Rose hurried to secure her belongings in time to add her small suitcase to the load; if she missed it, she would be forced to carry it to their next destination. After the accident, there was little chance her one good arm could manage the weight or the distance.

Hurriedly, she did a final check of her horse's stall, then went in search of her daughter. Wicker never strayed far from the tent even though she knew Rose would always find her. Rose spied the telltale bits of popcorn trailing across the lawn; Wicker's fondness for the traditional circus treat was surpassed only by her devotion to her mother, the bareback rider.

Rose quickened her step. Night would be upon them soon and neither of them could withstand the cold for more than a few minutes once the sun dropped out of sight. Already, the evening's chill seeped deep into her bones as she pulled the useless shawl more tightly about her rounded shoulders.

"Stop slouching," her mother's scornful voice criticized, "No man is going to look twice your way if you're a hunchback." Rose shook her head, the loose curls of her tresses dancing down her back, keeping the ghosts at bay for the night.

Wicker peered around the corner of the main tent at the sound of Rose's approach, blinking and breathing in shallow takes, the asthma squeezing her lungs as she scurried to Rose's side.

"He's gone, isn't he?" she sighed. "Are you ever going to tell Daddy who I am?"

3rd Place Winner: Infinite Pathways Flash Fiction

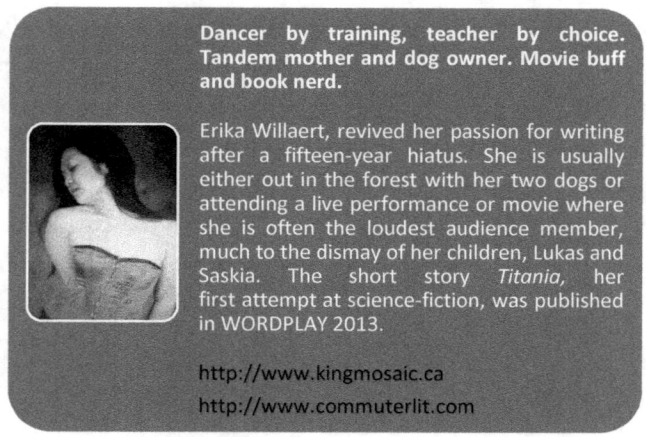

Dancer by training, teacher by choice. Tandem mother and dog owner. Movie buff and book nerd.

Erika Willaert, revived her passion for writing after a fifteen-year hiatus. She is usually either out in the forest with her two dogs or attending a live performance or movie where she is often the loudest audience member, much to the dismay of her children, Lukas and Saskia. The short story *Titania*, her first attempt at science-fiction, was published in WORDPLAY 2013.

http://www.kingmosaic.ca
http://www.commuterlit.com

The Nature of Infection

By Corrie Adams

Our bed is as old as our marriage and, after seventeen years, it sags in the middle and the springs creak like swollen joints.

Bryan rolls away from me, seeking higher ground. His breathing is the loudest thing in the room now that his heartbeat no longer thunders in my ear. The space between each inhale and exhale grows and I wonder if he's fallen asleep.

I peek at him through lowered lashes, he has thrown one arm across his face. It's a tanned arm, muscles trimmed with golden hair, and I know it well. Or I used to, anyway.

I reach over, run my hand along his flesh, attempting to relearn what has somehow been forgotten. A subtle twitch meets my fingertips, tension running just beneath his skin.

Not asleep, then.

I pull back.

The curtains tug against the rod as the breeze picks up. Sunlight sneaks in around the edges and I study the unfamiliar shadows. Lying down in the middle of the day is something I haven't done since college, when I spent a week in bed with pneumonia. Alone in my dorm room, I listened to the world outside moving on without me. It hurt to breathe.

Memories of that mid-afternoon solitude must be why the buzz of distant lawn mowers leaves me feeling so empty, and the smell of fresh-cut grass catches in my throat like tears, unshed.

Fevered and aching, then and now, I contemplate the nature of infection. Today, there is a "For Sale" sign marring our green lawn, but unlike my bout with pneumonia, this can't be cured with a round of antibiotics.

"The kids will be home soon," I say.

"Yes," he replies. He draws a breath; I picture a syringe, the cold point on the verge of puncturing flesh, and brace myself. But the jab doesn't come. Instead, he slips out of bed and begins to dress. I sink deeper into the dip in the centre.

"I've got to go," he says.

"The kids?"

"I'll call them."

"Stay," I say. "Please?"

"I'll see them Saturday." He pauses at the bedroom door, runs a hand through his hair and sighs. "Nothing's changed, Sarah."

"Everything has changed." I grab at the bed sheets, close my fists tightly in their folds to stop my hands from shaking.

"You'll sign the papers?"

I glance at the manila envelope I threw on the floor right before I kissed him.

"Yes," I say through lips that still sting with the memory. "I'll sign them."

He nods once, then again. He slips through the door. He doesn't look back.

Honourable Mention: Infinite Pathways Flash Fiction

Corrie spends her days wrangling numbers, but enjoys playing with words at night. Her work has appeared in magazines such as More of Our Canada and Lifestyles Magazine, and her short fiction has been included in several anthologies, including Renaissance: Short Fiction as selected by Sarah Selecky, and Little Bird Stories, volume 5.

Corrie lives in Newmarket, Ontario with her two sons and an overactive imagination.

The Decision

By Nancy Thorne

Dave sobbed behind me; the weight of the realization that his friend had passed away was too heavy to constrain. I thought for a moment of consoling him, but knew better. We all knew better as we sat and pretended the room was silent.

Ten minutes felt endless before the cremation coordinator finally entered and stood reverently with a binder clutched to his chest. My first impression was that he should enter an Elvis look-alike contest, but decided not to press on with that thought (except for the few seconds when I envisioned a swatch of his black hair careening down his forehead). I posed in pensive stillness and waited for the information he was about to spell out.

The range of crematory vessels was quite extensive, Elvis explained by rote while shifting his gaze over each of us, not certain who would make the final choice and therefore, supply payment.

I rotated my head nonchalantly to the side to see if I could spot Dave, but could only catch a glimpse of his reflection from the chrome paper towel dispenser on the wall. His head down, Dave accepted the tissue offered by the receptionist. Relief swept through me as the keening subsided to a muted sniffle and his face came up, dry.

I turned around and looked at him. He straightened his spine.

"Ready to make the decision?" I asked.

"Damn straight," he replied. "She was one hell of a cat."

 Nancy Thorne began her lifelong goal of becoming a writer in 2011 after retiring to the town of Whitby with her husband, two sons and a yellow lab.

Read It … and Rant

By Elaine Coish

"In the third stage of labour, you might feel some discomfort."

I glommed onto that one phrase with the hope and trust of the wide-eyed innocent. It was the 70s. I was pregnant. I read everything and anything I could get my hands on. This particular book was pithy and perky and I believed it.

And then I gave birth.

"*Might* feel some discomfort". Don't you love that word "might"? Not, I *will* feel, but I *might*. Like there's a possibility I won't. In the third stage of labour. Said with an absolutely straight face.

And *discomfort*. Another word that pooh-poohs reality. *Discomfort*. Discomfort is a hangnail. Discomfort is your leg falling asleep. Discomfort is an itch you can't reach. Discomfort does not register on the Richter Scale of Stage Three Labour.

Did I mention that I believed this stuff? Did I mention that I entered battle blithely unaware? Did I mention that fairy tales and bedtime stories weren't yet on my agenda?

It was the first time I realized that not everything I read was true. I'm not talking about National Enquirer here. This was a manual, a teaching tool, an aid aimed at educating the uninitiated.

Since that long-ago epiphany, my radar pings when I come across airy claims proliferating the media and promises of customer service reps - especially if followed by an exclamation mark, visual or implied. The cheque's in the mail. Make it tonight and wear it tomorrow. Wash and go haircut. Restores tooth enamel. No more cellulite. No more deadheading petunias. And my personal favourite, One size fits all.

Good PR will continue to ensnare the unsuspecting naïf, and I must admit there are times I've fallen prey to the siren's lure of a miracle, swayed by an ad's lofty declarations. Now, though, when I hear I've won a free trip to the Bahamas, I mutter, "Un-huh. And pigs fly."

Back to the halcyon days of my pregnancy for a moment. I also recall the movies they ran for us in the parenting class. Old, scratchy films from the early 60s they were, played on one of those pull-up white screens that never seemed big enough to contain the movie without much fiddling and finagling and inching the projector back until, voila!, synchronization. This one featured bouffant hairdos and nervous husbands pacing. The mom-to-be in full make-up fluttered her false eyelashes. Brave little smiles earned her pats of encouragement from gallant hubby.

Then came the wee wince to signal her discomfort. Guess she was in the third stage of labour.

An inaugural member of Writers' Ink at the Caledon Public Library and a graduate of York University and Mount Saint Vincent University, Halifax, Elaine Coish is an avid poet and short story writer.

Tick Tock

By MJ Moores

Feet hurried by: booted heels, galoshes, loafers, runners, and work boots. They beat the ground according to their own time. The small package wrapped in metallic blue paper, surrounded by a simple off-white silk ribbon remained unnoticed.

"Ding, ding, ding," sounded the warning bell as some feet exited and others entered the station.

The shiny blue package sat just under a worn wood-slotted bench by the wall, nearly hidden behind the front concrete leg. A loud whoosh sounded as a series of doors slid shut and the whirr of an electric motor, all ready stressed, hailed the start of another work day.

Still the package remained undisturbed.

Had someone taken the time to tie their shoe or pick up the rumpled newspaper lying on the seat of the bench, they might have heard a faint rhythmic tick, tick, tick speaking to itself inside the little blue box.

If only someone had taken the time to notice.

The clock on the painted-chipped cinder block wall tracked the time in wait of the next train. Footsteps clicked and clunked up and down broad, life-stained concrete stairs. A wail grew louder as a mother and her children tumbled onto the subterranean platform. She bounced the bundled baby in her arms and held fast to the toddler's mitten.

But the boy had wandered over to the old bench and crouched to look under – one hand mitted, the other not. He cocked his head to one side. The digital clock on the wall marked another minute gone. His mother looked frantically over her shoulders, clutching the small blue mitten.

The boy reached under the bench.

A university graduate of Theatre Production with a minor in Creative Writing and a BEd, MJ cannot help but combine her passions for the makebelieve and bring them to life both on the page and on the stage. http://mjmoores.com

Lost

By Corrie Adams

On the day Edward presented her with a brand new label-maker, Denise left a trail of Post-it notes behind her in crisscrossing trails all through the house. She tossed them to the ground in a colourful, over-sized confetti celebration. They said things like DISH SOAP and BANDAGES and SPOONS.

Their impermanence, the way the adhesive gradually lost its stickiness, had always bothered her. But now, she wouldn't need to worry that the Post-it for TOWELS might be blown off by an errant breeze, nor fret that the one reading CRACKERS would be accidentally swapped with the one that said PANTYHOSE. They would all be replaced with long-lasting, white strips of plastic.

She spent the evening labelling the kitchen (COFFEE MAKER, SPATULA, FLOUR) and the living room (STEREO, PHOTOGRAPHS, TV REMOTE). That night, she lay beside Edward and fell into a deep sleep. She dreamed it was storming and the power was out, but a fire burned in the hearth, dozens of candles illuminated the room, and she knew where everything was.

Early the next morning, she woke as Edward slipped out of bed. He kissed her, whispered "I love you", and dressed for work.

Denise listened to his car drive away and stretched, her limbs poking out from the blankets like question marks. The strip of light along the edge of the curtains reminded her of the label-maker.

She looked around their bedroom. The sight of all those tattered Post-it notes clinging to drawers and cupboards was an urgent call to action. She threw back the covers and arose.

But where was the label-maker?

Denise looked everywhere. She pawed through dresser drawers. She dumped out her sewing basket. She even hunted through the kitchen, pulling everything out of the pantry in the process. But she couldn't find her label-maker.

When Edward came home, he found Denise sitting on the floor among tins of soup and tuna fish, tears streaming down her cheeks.

"Sweetheart, what is it? Did you fall?"

"I lost it," she sobbed. "I lost the label-maker."

Edward took her hands, pulled her gently to her feet and led her to his desk. He opened the second drawer and there, nestled between the stapler and the packing tape, was her label-maker.

Her red-rimmed eyes begged Edward to return it to her. He nodded, but first he keyed in a few letters and then pressed the print button. He peeled off the backing and stuck the strip of plastic to the desk drawer: LABEL-MAKER.

Then he handed the machine to Denise. She hugged it to her chest and let out a shaky breath.

Edward was thankful the label-maker would help his wife navigate their home. But eventually, he knew, it wouldn't be enough. One day, the bold-faced type that spilled out would spell EDWARD and then everything would be lost, forever.

Corrie spends her days wrangling numbers, but enjoys playing with words at night. She lives in Newmarket, Ontario with her two sons and an overactive imagination.

Awareness
Fictional
Gritty Enjoying
Presence Light Discover
ShortStory Life
Universal
Dark Realistic
Encounter Empowering
Resilience

The Newfoundland Storyteller

By Anne Kathleen McLaughlin

This statue of the Virgin Mary, exquisitely sculpted by Giovanni Strazza of Milan, was imported from Rome in 1856. Note the sacred quality of the face, revealed and hidden by its marble veil.

E arly evening, the air so cool that I draw my sweater more closely around me, wish I'd worn socks in my sandals. As I walk towards the harbour, I wonder if it's nearness to the water that makes St. John's feel like Autumn in July. Maybe it's the distance I feel from home, from friends. I move towards the Storytelling like someone who moves closer to a campfire. Beside me, rows of wooden houses flaunt their colours with the wild joy of tulip fields: fuchsia, ochre, vermillion. I find Duckworth Street, and the Monument, climb the outdoor flight of rickety stairs to a shabby wooden door. I breathe, go inside.

I'm early, so I sit on a barstool and look around. This tiny dark room is the Crow's Nest Officers' Club. Around the walls are photos and mementos from hundreds of ships that have sailed into St. John's Harbour. I've arrived towards the end of another scheduled event. That blind man beside the fireplace is here to make a presentation to the club's master. I listen. He is one of two officers who made it out of the harbour alive after the sinking of his ship in the Second World War. The framed letter he holds is a citation for bravery. I can see his reluctance to let it go, to let go of the stories he wants to tell now of how it was in the icy waters, only his greatcoat keeping him from freezing to death. As the officer takes his leave, receiving a handshake in exchange for his treasure, the audience for the Storytelling is beginning to crowd in.

The Newfoundlander who approaches the wooden story stool beside the fire is young, perhaps just twenty. He sits unsmiling, looking somewhere beyond us, already in the realm of story. He takes us with him in a dory, and we see the muscles in his back straining with the pull of the oars as he turns into a cove, at the base of a steep hill. We struggle up the hill with him to a weathered grey wooden shack, pass through the open door. Old Eddy Greaves, deaf and weak, lies on a couch against the far wall. He is alone here, and yet through the window we see the garden with a wealth of vegetables, indoors the neatly stacked firewood, the fish prepared for frying. We cook his meal, and Eddy rises to eat with us. But suddenly utter darkness overcomes the house. With a great roar the sea rushes up the hillside, washes over the house. Then as quickly as it has come, it recedes into peaceful quiet. Our anxious eyes, gazing down into the cove, take in the sight of our dory rocking safely at anchor. With amazement we see that the sea has left fish and firewood, that the garden is covered with a rich fertilization of fish bones and sea plants. Eddy Greaves has a secret mother.

The young man stands, still unsmiling, returns to his place. There are other stories, spirits and ghosts who emerge from fog- shrouded graveyards; poetry funny and sad; even a teller from England who knows all the lines of "Albert and the Lion". No one warms me like the young Newfoundlander.

I'm already part way down the stairs, when I feel his hand touch me lightly on the back. I turn to see him gazing intently. "You a visitor here?"

"Is it so obvious?"

"Yes. You looked keen, like these stories were new to you."

"They were. They are. I liked yours." Like seems too little a word.

"You like stories, you should try the ghost walk."

"Sort of a scary thing for a woman alone." I feel a total fool as soon as I say it. I am old enough to be his mother. Maybe his grandmother.

"Come with me if you like." He extends a hand and I take it. "I'm Simon."

Night has fallen, a velvet blackness without moon. We make our way to the Anglican Cathedral of St. John the Baptist, where the Haunted Hike begins. The tall bearded storyteller has a great booming voice that guides us, telling tales all the while, as we trek through dark lanes, up and down the multitude of stairways on the streets of St. John's. Our final stop is the house where a young bride awaited the return of her sailor husband, who had promised he would not die, would not leave her widowed. One night, a neighbour saw the entry of a bedraggled sailor, wet as though from a night in the sea. The wife was never seen again. A puddle of seawater and seaweed was found by her bed.

Afterwards, we find the closest Tim Horton's, both of us more than ready for a hot cappuccino.

"Tell me about you," I say once we're seated, "how did someone so young come to be focused on the old stories?"

"I'll do better than that. I'll show you, if you're free tomorrow."

He walks back with me to the convent where I am staying and asks me to meet him in front of The Rooms next morning.

I let myself into the quiet house, head up the wide carpeted stairway to my room. I am smiling. A date. At my age!

I sleep well, better than I have since I arrived. But in my dreams my own ghosts come calling. I am sitting in Tim Horton's in Ottawa drinking iced cappuccino. My dream self seems unaware that this must have happened long before Tim Horton had become the eponymous name for a coffee shop. Across from me is Mara, the luminous child who was for a time my student, then for many years my friend. She is smiling. I see again her sea green eyes with wisps of gold shells in their irises.

"I met your son, Simon, in St. John's," I tell her. Then suddenly she is gone. Seawater with bits of seaweed stains the chair where she sat.

The air is thick with fog when I wake up. I wonder if he'll be there, if he's found a better way to spend his day. But once I get close enough to the gigantic salt box of a building that is Art Gallery, Museum and Archives in one, I see him. He leads me to the first floor and without preamble gestures towards a squared pillar that serves as display wall for pieces of art. From about three feet away, I gaze at a bronze statuette. I notice the taut agony of the face, focused on a silent shout, the naked body with every muscle tightened to endure the hanging position. I look at how the hands are raised, fastened to a horizontal shape. I feel shock at first, but then a door opens inside me, "Why, it looks like…"

"No," he says, "Don't say anything. Just look."

I read the title: "Man nailed to fish."

On the wall adjacent there is a painting. I breathe in the colour and texture of the soft green woodland scene in which fish bones predominate. I keep looking until I see that the bones shape themselves into a crown of thorns over the brow of a man, his hand in his mouth as though to cut off a cry of agony. I begin to understand that seeing Newfoundland requires eyes like Mara's: eyes that have the depth of the sea within them, eyes that see beneath the fog shroud, the invisibility cloak.

Simon gestures towards the stairs. On the next level we find a temporary exhibit of Christopher Pratt's paintings. Here are his words, painted on the wall beside this house whose pale yellow light bravely opposes the fog-haunted landscape:

My strongest associations relate to qualities of light – the precise, recurring sense I get of things when they are lit in a certain way."

Absorbed by these paintings, I forget the silent presence of my guide. I gaze at "The Road to Venus", a huge dark highway allured by the solitary silver light of a distant planet. I notice in painting after painting how the light and the lovely beckoning earth call out to whoever is barricaded in square houses and behind cross-barred windows. I see how the light continually is cast in the role of David in the face of Goliath darkness.

Pratt's 1969 painting, "Shop on an Island" tells of the resettlement that followed Newfoundland's entry into Confederation in 1949. I look first at the painting, feel the desolation of the empty shelves before I read the words:

Seemingly overnight, there were abandoned villages all around the coast. People just packed up and left, leaving behind their ways and means of life,

after towing their houses behind their boats like huge windowless whales. In many places only a few larger buildings remained, churches and schools and shops. They were like well-formed ships mysteriously abandoned at sea: sound, seaworthy, but with no sign of crew. They stood as memorials until wanderers and the weather tore them down.

I walk to the window of the second storey stairwell, look down at St. John's. The window bars, like the ones in Pratt's painting, create a cross that hangs protectively over the city. The fog outside obscures the light so it is my own reflection that looks back at me, joined by a ghostly Simon at my shoulder, tears in his eyes refracting light like tiny crystals.

When we emerge, Simon asks whether I've seen the art treasure the convent has. "It's called the Veiled Virgin, brought here from Italy in the 19th Century. The artist was able to sculpt it so the face is visible through a veil of marble."

I admit that someone offered to let me see it, but I hadn't been interested. His tone is deprecating, his face solemn: "Have you heard about the Upper Canadian who missed the greatest piece of art in St. John's?" It takes a heartbeat before I get it. The Newfoundlander's version of the Newfie joke.

"Come. I have a good friend who'll give us a private viewing. It's one of her jobs to take tourists to see the sculpture."

Sister Magdalena, summoned by a bell that chimes deep in the building, is in her mid-seventies. She looks ordinary enough, until her eyes rest on Simon. Then her face radiates light like one of Pratt's houses. I realize now that I've seen her at the breakfast table on two different mornings, but did not think to speak with her. She had a detached, almost grieving, air that set her apart, and asked for solitude.

But now she looks at me with interest. "You're the retired teacher from Ontario who's been here all week."

"Yes. This trip was a retirement gift. Were you also a teacher?"

"No. I cared for children in a Quebec orphanage until it closed some years ago. I transferred to this community because ... I had, have, family here."

"She'd like to see the Veiled Virgin. Is this a good time?"

In its glass case in the private chapel sits a snow white face of incredible delicacy. The veil is a wisp of air, a morning fog, a blessing across her beauty. We stand rapt for a long time.

Later, after Sister Magdalena leads us back to the outer door, she embraces each of us. With a shy smile she tells us that it might be time for her to retire from this task since only that morning one of the tourists said that the veiled lady looked like her!

Dinner would be my treat, to thank Simon for the tour. We choose an Irish pub on George Street, order thick battered cod steaks and fries. I am sitting across from him as the evening light from the window creates green jewels in his dark eyes. Startled, I recall my dream.

"What's wrong?" he asks. "You look like you've seen a ghost."

I continue to look. Finally, I say, "I think I have."

He has the grace to wait.

"I had a student once. Brilliant. When she was eleven, she introduced me to *The Lord of the Rings*, brought each hardback volume in turn for me to read. She was reading

Plato at the age of sixteen, had decided to become a Quaker. She married, had a son. Each summer when I returned to Ottawa we'd walk along the canal, talk about books, relationships, God. You remind me of her."

He grins, "Maybe I'm her lost son who ran off to sea…"

"No. Her son died in an accident before he was two. She never got over the grief. A few years later, she took her own life. I've never stopped missing her."

Suddenly, I am weeping as I have not done in years. For Mara, for loss, for beauty, intelligence, goodness. For the end of my teaching years.

A hand is warm over my own where it rests on the table. Two green-flecked eyes search mine. "You have no children of your own?"

"I'm a nun," I say.

At this he looks startled, and I feel a sharp regret that the thread woven between us will snap. Slowly, he smiles. "My grandmother was … well, *is* … a nun."

He tells me that his grandmother had lived on one of Pratt's isolated fishing islands near Trinity. Brought to the mainland in 1950 at the age of sixteen, along with many siblings, she was put into service as a housekeeper for a wealthy family and seduced by the eldest son, became pregnant. After her child, a girl, was born, her parents, through the intervention of their parish priest, took her to a convent in Quebec City where she was received as a novice.

"I grew up knowing nothing of this, of course. I only sensed in my mother a great sadness, was led to believe that her mother had died in childbirth. Two years ago, my mother died after a few months' illness. I found out the truth at the wake. By then, I was in my second year of university, taking a degree in History, planning to teach. I'll graduate next year. But once I knew the story, I started going to Trinity. I'll spend the rest of the summer there, telling tourists of the resettlement, all that's been lost."

"Sister Magdalena is your grandmother?" I ask, see the answer in his eyes.

Newfoundland, the veiled virgin, harsh, lovely, holding secrets in the roots of her ancient rocks, offering stories that nourish her people's spirits, teaching them to look for the light that the darkness will not overcome.

1st Place Winner: Infinite Pathways Short Story Competition

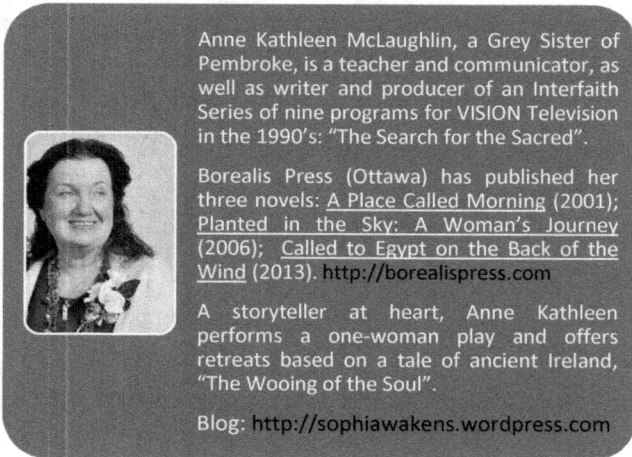

Anne Kathleen McLaughlin, a Grey Sister of Pembroke, is a teacher and communicator, as well as writer and producer of an Interfaith Series of nine programs for VISION Television in the 1990's: "The Search for the Sacred".

Borealis Press (Ottawa) has published her three novels: A Place Called Morning (2001); Planted in the Sky: A Woman's Journey (2006); Called to Egypt on the Back of the Wind (2013). http://borealispress.com

A storyteller at heart, Anne Kathleen performs a one-woman play and offers retreats based on a tale of ancient Ireland, "The Wooing of the Soul".

Blog: http://sophiawakens.wordpress.com

I Am, Apparently, a Slow Learner

~ a true story
By Chris Macgregor

L ife gives us recurring messages until we learn whatever it is that we need to learn. I've always thought that this is why I have eight children. God keeps giving us children until we get it right. Most people figure it out after two or three, but I am, apparently, a slow learner. In fact, I think God may have just given up on me because I am still not sure what it is I was supposed to have learned.

Having eight kids has mostly just made me tired and apathetic and I really can't see that being one of life's great truths. In all honesty, though, having eight children has taught me a few things. For instance, I can remove stains from almost anything, I can repair toys like one of Santa's elves and I never travel with my children unless I can bring drinks, food and sedatives, (for me not for the children).

The lesson never seems to sink in but one lesson that life continues to throw at me with eight children is, that you can't plan for everything. When I was pregnant with my first baby I envisioned sitting in a rocking chair, gently humming while my angelic baby dozed peacefully in my arms. Reality found me walking, pacing and jiggling a screaming hellion that never slept and made sure I never did either. Having a second child, I pictured them playing happily together while

I (inexplicably looking like June Cleaver) quietly knit in the background. Reality found me prying a stick from Joel's hand before he beat Kaity senseless and Kaity complaining because Joel had breathed on her.

Having eight children is nothing like the 'Brady Bunch' or 'Eight is Enough' – TV shows I watched as a kid. It's loud, chaotic and messy. Very, very messy. Being a bit of a clean freak, I've always struggled with this aspect of parenting a large family. I once saw a poster that read, "Cleaning the house when you have kids is like trying to brush your teeth while eating an Oreo cookie." That pretty much describes my life.

Yet, I still keep trying – not because the children care. They would live, knee-deep in garbage and not notice, but I can't relax in a messy room. I've tried various strategies to keep the house clean but as any parent knows, getting children to do chores is more work than actually doing the chore yourself. But then they'll never learn to clean up after themselves and be responsible human beings. Right? Besides, I might actually want to visit them when they (God willing) someday move out and get a place of their own because (God willing) I'll still be alive and my grandchildren will be living with them.

So, because I am a slow learner, I keep trying. Over the years I have tried many different strategies to get the children to help out with chores; with varying degrees of success. I have tried incentive programs, actually quite similar to Air Miles or other rewards systems that stores use. When the child does a chore they receive points towards some kind of reward. These systems worked well … at first but eventually they all failed. I think there were several reasons for this: 1) At first the kids would go crazy doing chores and I ran out of whatever reward I was offering; and 2) Kids lose interest quickly so you have to keep upping the ante; and 3) Unlike the Air Miles people, I don't have a staff and computer system to track said points and the upkeep of the system became more difficult than actually doing the chores.

I've tried several confiscation programs, again with limited success. Basically, if I found something lying around, I'd take it and put it in a bin that, each night, was emptied into another bin out in the garage. The theory behind this plan was that the children would get tired of having to go out to the garage to look for their stuff and learn to put things away. It's a nice idea but unfortunately, flawed. It's based on the premise that kids will think about the future ramifications of their present behaviour. These are kids we are talking about. They don't think that far ahead. In fact, my children loved this system. They could leave stuff anywhere and everywhere and they would always know where to find it later.

This system worked better when I changed it to a bin hidden in my room and they had to do a chore to get their stuff back. In fact, this system worked so well, that I was having a hard time thinking up chores for them to do to. For the most part they don't leave anything lying around my living room anymore, but they know that I won't bother going down to the rec room, so everything seems to accumulate there. I don't really mind this trade off since that's their space and I avoid it like the plague. However, it does become an issue when I have to circumnavigate my way to the laundry room through the mountains of toys, clothes, electronics and dirty dishes. It is a perilous journey and not for the faint of heart.

Getting the kids to actually clean up the house is a constant battle. At least once a week the house gets a deep cleaning. By that I mean really, deep down cleaning—especially the bathroom since, with boys in the house, I have to clean around the toilet every single time I go in there. Having never been a boy or had the option of peeing from a standing position, I don't really know the process, but it seems to me that it shouldn't actually be that difficult to get the pee into the toilet. I mean, seriously, it is a pretty big target. What the hell are my boys doing in there? The hokey-pokey? I don't know how they even have enough pee to get that kind of coverage. So, once a week we do a deep cleaning.

Up until recently, I had chore schedules but as the kids have grown, it's been more difficult to maintain. There always seems to be one or more kids missing and it's unfair (not to mention impossible to enforce) to make a kid do the dishes when they weren't home for dinner in the first place. This, often, left me with one or more chores that no one wanted to cover. The whining, complaining and negotiations that ensued led to my needing serious therapy and a lawyer on retainer.

In desperation, I stumbled upon a system that not only solved the problem of delegating the chores but also taught my children another lesson; the dangers of gambling. I took an old deck of cards and wrote the chores on the card faces. After every meal it's a simple matter of dealing out the cards. Whoever cooked doesn't get a card and the rest of the cards are dealt out to whoever ate. There's still complaining and some tears but it's the luck of the draw and you just can't argue with that. Everyone hates getting the wash or dry cards and if someone complains that they've got a dishes card three times in a row, I just say, "And this is why you should never gamble."

At some point, I guess I decided that being a single mom with eight kids just wasn't messy enough because, four years ago I let Joel and Emily talk me into getting a kitten. Up until that time, I always responded to the request for pets with a resounding, "No! There are far too many animals living in this house already."

Over the years, the kids all asked for different pets. Kaity was particularly keen on getting a parrot. At one point, she'd nagged me about it for so long that I finally said, "Fine we can get a parrot, already."

"Really?!" She said, with a comically shocked look on her face. Hardly daring to believe her ears.

"Yes," I sighed defeated, "but, you'll have to move out, because there's only so much room." That ended the requests for a parrot.

When Joel was around fourteen, he talked me into

allowing him to slowly torture a beta fish to death. He didn't sell it to me in quite that manner. However, in the end that's what happened.

"Beta fish are called Chinese fighter fish, Mom," he informed me. "They are really easy to take care of, Mom. I just need a little tank and no heater or aerator or anything. I'll feed it and they are really neat. If I put a mirror in front of the tank it will get angry and try to fight," he said. Then he threw in the age old promise, "You won't have to take care of it at all, Mom, I'll do everything."

So I, rather naively, purchased a beta fish and "starter kit" from the pet store. It was indeed a beautiful fish. It sat on the kitchen counter and Joel did feed it, and watch it and put mirrors in front of its tank to make it "fight". When this became boring, he bought another tank with a female and proceeded to try to breed them. This resulted in the female getting damn near killed several times, and then Joel lost interest in the fish completely. The female was the first to die (I'm not sure if it was from lack of feeding or if she finally succumbed to the wounds inflicted by the male). The male hung on for almost another year.

Now the death of a pet can be a learning experience but also painful for a child. When Joel's first fish died, Kaity and her boyfriend Sean were the first to discover the "tragic demise" and pondered how best to break the news to Joel.

They sat Joel down and very solemnly Kaity said, "Joel we have something important to tell you."

But, Joel seemed to guess what she was going to say and a look of pure horror came across his face. "Oh my God! You're pregnant!" he exclaimed.

Now, it was Kaity who was horrified, "What?! No! Of course not!"

Sean stepped in and calmly directed Joel's attention to the fish floating at the top of the tank, "No, Joel. Your fish died."

Joel glanced over at the tank and, clearly unimpressed, said, "Oh. Yeah."

Kaity was now lacking any sympathy for him at all and asked, "That's it?"

Matter-of-factly, Joel told her, "Well, I figured she was going to die soon. She hasn't eaten for days."

Kaity just shook her head and walked away muttering, "Whatever."

After Joel's fish died, I was hoping we were done with the whole fish episode but Hannah talked me into letting *her* get a beta fish. His name was "Bubbles" and he was the only ugly beta fish in the store, so, naturally, that was the one that Hannah wanted. I think she felt sorry for him or maybe he was beautiful to her (love is blind). Anyway, (ugliness notwithstanding) Bubbles lasted almost two years before succumbing to the neglect and passing on to the great sewage plant in the beyond, and I announced that we had tortured enough fish.

I thought that was the end of our days as pet owners, but I was wrong. A couple of years later, Joel's friend's cat had kittens. I don't know if it was just a weak moment or if it was the combination of Joel and Emily both working me at the same time, but I agreed to "just go look at" the kittens. Folks, take it from me, never, ever agree to "just go look at" whatever baby animal your child is begging you to take in. This is a trap! You will succumb. God has purposely made all baby animals (including humans) look adorable so that you will be unable to resist loving them and agreeing to take care of them. However, they will quickly grow up and no longer be adorable but you will still have to take care of them.

There were four kittens in the litter. Kaity convinced her husband, Sean, to "just go look at them", and they took one home, (see my above warning). There were three of the cutest little fur balls left. Joel and Emily chose one and I decided that it would be lonely on its own, (lonely in a house with seven kids? What was I thinking?). So, I chose one of his brothers to keep him company. This left just one little kitten, on its own. I almost broke down and took that one too, but I convinced another friend to "just go look at it" and she took it home with her.

So, now we were the proud owners of Jazz and Megatron (these names are, apparently from the movie *Transformers*. Clearly chosen by the children.). I called them Jazz and Meg. They were the cutest little things but at first they were, seriously, as much work as a newborn. I was up at night with them. One had trouble adjusting to solid food and pooped everywhere. They were a huge pain in the ass but the kids adored them. We have more pictures of the cats on our computer than of the kids.

Now, naturally, the kids told me that they would do all the work. They would feed them, clean the litter box and clean up after them. And, of course, that has never happened. I have always been the one to feed them and clean up after them. And there has been a lot of cleaning.

Jazz, as previously mentioned, had bowel issues for the first few weeks and Meg would eat anything. And I do mean anything. He ate rubber bands, balloons, plastic bottle caps, tape and ribbons. This wouldn't have been so bad, except that he would then puke the items up (accompanied by an entire can of half digested food) all over the house. For some strange reason that scientists have yet to explain (probably because they aren't actually researching it) kids cannot see a huge mound of cat vomit. They will instinctively step over it, but when you point it out and ask them why they didn't clean it up, they will tell you that they didn't see it. And apparently, they still can't see it because they will walk away and leave it there for you to clean up, unless you threaten them with death or no Wi-Fi access.

As with the fish, owning a cat does, often, lead to the issue of dealing with the death of a pet. Except that unlike the death of a fish, the death of a cat is traumatic and expensive. As mentioned, Meg would eat anything. He and Jazz were "indoor" cats but Meg liked to escape outside. With seven kids coming and going, this was easily done. One day Meg returned and promptly began to puke up some kind of bright yellow substance (I suspect it was anti-freeze but it could have been pretty much anything). Whatever the substance was, it caused Meg to get very, very sick. He didn't eat (which caused him to stop puking but isn't a very good long term solution). He got thinner and thinner and it became apparent that he wasn't going to get over this on his own. Now I had to make a choice. Do I take the cat to the vet? Folks, vets are expensive. I'm sure they deserve the fees but, and this is a big but, when you're a single mom with seven kids at home, you cannot afford to pay a huge vet bill. I finally gave in and took Meg to the vet.

The very official man in the white lab coat informed me in a very serious voice, "Ma'am this is a very sick cat. To really do this up right would require tests, an IV and we would need to keep him here in our hospital facility."

I didn't want to seem cold but that all sounded like, "Blah, blah, blah ... expensive." So, trying not to sound cold-hearted, I asked, "Um, well ... how much would that cost?"

"You would be looking at around $1500, today. Then tomorrow we will look at the test results and assess how much more it will cost," he informed me.

I just narrowly avoided shouting out, "Are you out of your freakin' mind?" and managed to answer in what I hoped was a civil voice, "Well, no offense but I am a single mom. There is really no way I can afford $1500."

To his credit, he didn't bat an eyelash or look the least bit condescending when he offered an alternative, "Well, a more conservative route would be to do some blood work and give him some medication to settle his stomach. Then reassess tomorrow."

I, rather naively, thought that this would be relatively inexpensive, so I agreed. "Ok, yeah that sounds good."

So $400 later, blood samples had been taken and I took Meg home with some medication. Now, as I understand it, giving a dog medication is a fairly easy process. Wrap the pill in some meat, offer to dog, dog eats, repeat as necessary. Getting a cat to take a pill, even a cat that is very weak and on the brink of death, is infinitely more difficult. It's going to take a considerable amount of time and involve several people willing to sustain multiple scratches and bites. After a long and injurious battle, we managed to get Meg to swallow the pill, only to have him puke it back up. At which point, I decided it was cruel to torture him any longer and let him rest.

I called the vet the next morning. Meg's kidneys and liver had shut down. There was no hope. The only humane thing to do was to bring Meg in and have him put down (this, by the way, costs another $300). Now, this is one of the things I hate about being a single mom. You have to do these types of things on your own. In retrospect, I could have saved myself a lot of money and grief. Meg was so close to dying that I should have let him die at home with a whole lot more dignity. But I didn't want to be inhumane; so I explained to the kids, let them say their tearful, heartbroken goodbyes and took him to the vet to do the "humane" thing.

Only, I am still not sure what part of the process was "humane". Taking him in to be put down saved him only hours of suffering and caused me trauma that I'll never get over. All I'm going to say is, if you are having a pet put down, don't go in. I felt guilty about just handing Meg over to die "alone". He was barely a year old, just a kitten. So I opted to stay with him until it was over. This was a horribly traumatic experience that I will never, ever repeat. It was nothing like the wonderfully touching scene I'd seen in the movie *Marley and Me* and, in fact, was far more like a morgue scene from *Criminal Minds*.

Then there were the kids to go home to with the empty cat carrier. They were heartbroken; almost as heartbroken as Jazz who never understood and now, absolutely refuses to ever go anywhere in that cat carrier. Then we talked about the fact that at least Meg wasn't suffering anymore (the kids and I; Jazz didn't seem to want to talk about it).

So after Meg died, I was quite content to have just one cat. I realized that with seven kids in the house, Jazz was anything but lonely. However, Kaity felt so bad about Meg that, two months later, she bought Emily a cat for Christmas. She was a black cat named Minnie that Kaity found in a no kill shelter (upon arrival she found that a no kill shelter, or at least this particular no kill shelter, was a crazy cat lady with around one hundred cats). The kids named her Narcissa (the cat, not the crazy cat lady). I believe this time the name was derived from the *Harry Potter* movies. I can hardly wait to see what my grandchildren are named. She is a short-haired, black cat that they said was around five years old. She is good natured and she and Jazz get along. The only problem with her is that she seems to be allergic to cats (at least that is my theory). She's always sneezing and wheezing and has a 'runny nose'. I thought cleaning up cat vomit was bad but you would not believe how difficult it is to clean up cat snot. I think that NASA should research the uses of cat snot, 'cos seriously folks, once that stuff gets on a wall or the furniture, it is never, ever coming off.

So Narcissa is small and dainty. Jazz on the other hand is huge and, as I discovered, a very good hunter. I have an irrational fear of rodents or "creepy crawlies" of any kind and unfortunately, all of my children have inherited (learned?) this behaviour. Before Jazz and Meg joined the family, we had a problem with mice. When I heard the little devils scurrying around in the dining room, I immediately (after hyperventilating and generally freaking out) bought some mouse traps, set them up under the dining room hutch where no one would accidentally trip them, and congratulated myself on my superior intelligence. However, the next morning when we checked the traps and discovered three dead mice, I realized that I'd made a grave error. No one, least of all me, wanted to reach under the hutch to retrieve the little critters.

I tried bribing the kids with money and junk food, to no avail. Eventually, I put on some big gardening gloves and swept them out with a broom. Between bouts of the heebie-jeebies, I managed to get them into a trash bag and out into the trash bins in the garage. At this point, Tim pointed out to me that I was supposed to take the mice out of the traps and re-use them, (the traps, not the mice). I just stared at him speechlessly and walked away. Clearly, traps were not the right solution for me. Another trip to the hardware store and I returned with Warfarin. Again I placed it under the hutch, away from curious children. Warfarin is quite literally rat poison and as I understand it you sprinkle the poison on food, (I used bacon bits), the mice eat the food, (and the poison) and die. This sounded good to me, as long as they died somewhere other than under my hutch.

This plan worked great, except for one problem. If you manage to poison a mouse and she has a nest in your wall, the babies will eventually die as well, and a nest full of dead baby mice smells really, really, vile. In fact, it smells so bad that you will have to vacate your house until the smell dissipates (in our case for around 10 days).

But this was all before I had cats. So how did I find out that Jazz was a hunter? Well, at first, there were little clues. He would chase, and eventually eat any fly, spider or bug that managed to, very unwisely, enter the house. It was kind of gross, but hey, at least I didn't have to kill it, right? However, one day a chipmunk managed to find its way into the house. Not one child would own up to leaving the door open, so I can only conclude that the chipmunk actually opened the door on its own and walked in. Now chipmunks are cute, right? My kids love watching them in the yard, but the minute one gets into the house, it's no longer cute. It's a rodent. There was complete chaos; screaming and yelling and standing on furniture (and that was just me). We tried to 'herd' him as it were, back out the front door but the terrified little thing hid under the entertainment centre in the living room and no amount of 'coaxing' would get him out.

The kids were trying to lure the chipmunk into a pail and take it back outside when I remembered that we owned a cat. I suggested that we let Jazz chase it out. They could then trap it and "voila" problem solved. Emily pointed out that Jazz might actually catch the chipmunk and kill it but I disregarded this suggestion with a laugh.

"He's a big old house cat," I said scoffing. "He's not going to be able to catch it. He'll just chase it out and then you can trap it."

So I brought Jazz downstairs and placed him in front of the entertainment centre. I was wondering how to draw his attention to the chipmunk when he stopped dead, whipped his head around and stared directly at it. I had an inkling that my plan was flawed when he slowly looked up at me and smiled. I swear to God, that cat smiled at me in a "now that is the kind of toy I'm talkin' about" kind of way. And then he pounced, but it wasn't the chipmunk that ran out from under the television. It was Jazz with the chipmunk locked firmly in his jaws.

Unfortunately, he ran straight to me, and being the brave soul that I am, I immediately screamed like a girl and jumped up onto a chair and out of the way. The kids were horrified.

"Mom, he's going to kill it!" they cried. I was too shocked to move.

Emily, however, was like a Ninja. She grabbed Jazz and started swinging him around shouting, "Let it go! Let it go!" I can't imagine what this would have looked like to anyone who had the misfortune to wander into our house at that precise moment. All the kids were screaming, I was standing on a chair and Emily was swinging around a huge cat with a terrified chipmunk in its mouth. At this point Jazz, wisely (or mistakenly), did let go of the chipmunk and it literally flew across the living room, into the kitchen, where it promptly scurried under the stove out of Jazz's reach.

Now, when you are a single mom with eight kids, the ability to delegate isn't just a good idea, it is a necessity and I have become very, very good at delegating. It occurred to me at this moment that I was not the best "man" for this job. So, I took the little kids and Jazz upstairs and left Emily and her friend Ben to round up the chipmunk, which was a relatively fast and easy task once the room was emptied of screaming kids and menacing cats.

The chipmunk practically ran into the pail saying, "Holy shit! Get me out of this mad house!"

I think he may even have suggested to Emily and Ben that they would be wise to get out while they still could, too. And let's face it, some days I would gladly take that chipmunk's advice.

Some days, I look at the chaos that is my life and wander around muttering to myself, "Why on earth did I have all these kids? There is no sane reason to have this many kids." And it's true, unless you have a farm or family business that requires lots of free, child labour, there's just no sane reason to have a bunch of kids. The hours and pay suck, there's almost no vacation time and not much of a retirement plan either (hoping for one of the kids to make it big and take care of me in my old age, isn't so much a retirement plan as a huge gamble). And yet, strangely, there is nothing else I would rather do with my life. Probably because I still haven't learned that lesson, life is trying to teach me.

2nd Place Winner: Infinite Pathways Short Story Competition

Chris Macgregor is a single mom with eight kids. She lives in Newmarket (a lovely town north of Toronto) where she is commonly referred to as 'the lady with all the kids'. In her spare time she loves to travel, camp, hike, read and take long walks on the beach...and she fully intends to do all of those things and more, once the kids have grown up and moved out. In the meantime, being a single mom, she doesn't have any spare time, so she enjoys cooking, cleaning, car-pooling and amateur medicine/ psychology.

e-Happiness

By Elaine Jackson

"You must be Eleanor" he said.

I was stunned. The cold air was still nestled in the fake fur around my collar and the snow dripped off my boots onto the salt-stained ceramic tile.

"I came here to meet Eric," I said, trying to mentally compute who this stranger might be and how he would know my name. The coffee shop bustled with Saturday morning hipsters, most of whom gazed at their laptops and cell phones.

"I *am* Eric," he said. And the crowds of voices in my head began to murmur: *We told you. Everybody told you. Internet dating is a stupid idea and only fit for the desperate*. I stood, frozen, with a drooping sensation in my chest, somewhere between embarrassment and anger.

"Will you at least sit down?" My voices and I slumped into the metal chair he held out for me, which scraped noisily against the dirty floor. I tried to gather myself together.

"I'm sorry," I finally managed to say; "You look nothing like your picture."

"That's because the picture is about thirty years old—I just haven't gotten round to having another one taken. My wife always said it was the best picture I ever took."

"So you're married as well?"

"Widowed."

I wasn't sure whether to be less horrified or more.

"Would you like a coffee?" he asked.

"I guess." I mentally tallied the two hours I'd spent choosing my wardrobe, getting dressed, undressed and redressed, curling my hair, putting on makeup, taking the subway and then another half an hour wandering up and down the frozen street trying not to be early. For this. For him. He owed me a coffee.

"What do you take in it?"

"I'd like some whiskey," I said.

"I like you already."

"I was joking," I said. "I want cream. Lots of cream. No sugar."

He climbed slowly out of his chair and limped slightly on his way to the chrome and granite counter. His tweed jacket and jeans stood out shabbily against the black clad, tattooed, fashionable clientele. The barista glanced over at me curiously. I tried to imagine the best excuse I could come up with for bolting after the coffee. I probably should have bolted already. I still could, I thought, but that would be mean and I might regret it later. He was an old man. I could at least be temporarily pleasant. He must be lonely. I watched surreptitiously as he chatted amiably with the barista, and I strained to hear them over the noisy grinding and hissing of the cappuccino machine. The aroma of coffee grounds and chocolate warmed me a little.

By the time Eric returned with my coffee I'd removed my bulky parka, but left my scarf on to hasten my exit.

He grinned at me, "I take it you've never done this before?"

"I've had blind dates before, but never with someone who could be my granddad."

"Ouch," he said. But he didn't look deterred. "I thought you might have brought along your dog."

"My dog doesn't drink coffee," I said, "and besides, no one meets my dog on the first date. Did you bring yours?" I hadn't noticed any dogs parked outside.

"I didn't. I don't like to get his hopes up."

"Oh," I said. This was really awkward. And weird. Exponentially more awkward and weird than I'd been expecting. I pressed my palms into my coffee cup hoping it could sustain me, wishing the caffeine could speed up the minutes instead of my heart rate.

He sighed. "We were such a good match on e-Happiness."

"Obviously there was one large detail you chose to leave out."

"Does it really matter?"

"Yes, Eric. I know that it's shallow perhaps, but yes, it

does matter. I can't be in love with someone your age. I just can't imagine it."

He smiled then. Not the reaction I was expecting.

"I think you're prettier in person than in your profile picture." He leaned back as if to get a better view.

"Thank you. That doesn't change my feelings about second date potential here."

A chunk of white hair had fallen across his brow and I realized that the man had copious amounts of hair. He must once have been very handsome—in fact I could, when I really looked, still see the fellow in the thirty-year-old picture. His hands rested gently on the table, and he seemed completely at ease in his body; a serenity I found enviable and likeable.

"So I'm thinking that technically you must be some sort of quasi-pedophile. I realize that I'm past the age of consent but I don't have the looks or the temperament to be trophy wife material, so what were you thinking?"

He laughed. He laughed for a long time. People were staring. He finally composed himself. "I have a young fellow, probably your age, who helps me with odd jobs. We were talking one day and he explained to me that this is how dating is done these days. I thought it might be a lark. We went to the library and set the whole thing up on his laptop. Victor told me that I should put my age in according to the age of the woman I wanted to meet. So I aimed high, or low depending on how you look at it. I thought what the hell...

nothing's going to come of it anyway. But then you answered my message and I figured since I was on this train, I may as well wait and see where it goes. And here we are."

"But that's not the point," I said. "You brought me here under false pretences. I thought I was meeting a forty-year-old architect."

"I was an architect for forty years. I still do the odd drawing," he said.

"But this is not what I signed up for."

"Eleanor," he said, "How can you ever know what you signed up for? You get born, various pleasant and unpleasant things happen. You fall in love, you fall out of love, and next thing you know you're alone, your friends are dropping like flies and the only conversation anybody seems to make is related to knee replacements and colonoscopies. I'm tired of talking with people my age. They're all so damned old."

"Don't you have kids?"

"No. It didn't happen. And back then you either adopted or you just got on with your life. We got along all right."

"Surely there are easier ways to meet people than perpetrating fraud on e-Happiness?"

He grinned, "You're here aren't you? If it is so easy, why are you here?"

He had a point. "I'm here because I'm tired of people telling me that my life won't be complete until I have a man.

I'm tired of people telling me that I'm not trying hard enough. I'm tired of spending seventy percent of my income on rent and I'm tired of having roommates who move in single and then bring home a series of dates whom I either detest, envy, or worst of all fall in love with—only to have them move out on a moment's notice and leave me an apologetic note."

"So it's not really about sex then, is it?"

"Eric! That's a little personal. I'm surprised you'd ask such a thing."

"I'm old Eleanor, not dead."

"How old exactly? If that's not too personal …"

"I'm seventy-one."

I took a long sip of my coffee. "It's not about sex, but I think sex has to be involved somehow. I think it has to be the glue that holds the whole tenuous thing together. Or at least sets the foundation …"

"There are pills for that now you know."

"Except that before sex," I continued, thinking to myself that I can't believe I'm even having this conversation, "before sex, there has to be desire, and this is where this whole idea is breaking down for me."

"I expected as much." He fiddled with his coffee spoon and gazed at me wistfully. "This is only a first date. Don't you think you're moving a little fast?"

I blushed. I couldn't believe it but now he'd made me blush. "I appreciate the coffee, and I'm sure that you're a lovely person, you do have a dog after all. I had fun writing to you. But I don't need another roommate."

"I wouldn't leave," he said. "And I have a nice little house in High Park. I wouldn't expect sex and I wouldn't ask for much beyond a little companionship and some help around the house. Your dog would be so happy there. You could quit your job; pursue something else you would really like."

Part of me, the logical part, was starting to entertain this argument. I imagined walks in High Park, and introducing Eric to my friends. My parents would be horrified of course. Although maybe not. I'd given up trying to predict their reactions.

I was at a loss for words. I pulled my purse onto my lap and dug around for some lip gloss. My glasses, which I hadn't worn for reasons of vanity, tumbled to the floor and I ducked under the table to recover them. By the time I straightened up my hair was completely dishevelled and Eric reached across the narrow table to brush it away from my eyes. I let him. "Why me?" I said. "Why out of all the profiles in the 30-35 age range did you decide to pick me?"

He gazed at me softly for a moment. I noticed the green flecks in his large hazel eyes and imagined him lounging with the dogs in a room filled with light and paintings (mine). He drew in a breath and said, "To be honest, Eleanor, you're the spitting image of my wife … thirty years ago, I mean."

I winced and tightened my scarf around my neck. He glanced down at his hands. I took a final swig of my coffee and put on my coat. I stood up and deftly put my hand on his shoulder to prevent him from standing. He didn't even try.

"Thanks for the coffee Eric. I wish you luck." I kissed him on the crown of his head, picked up my bag, and went home.

3rd Place Winner: Infinite Pathways Short Story Competition

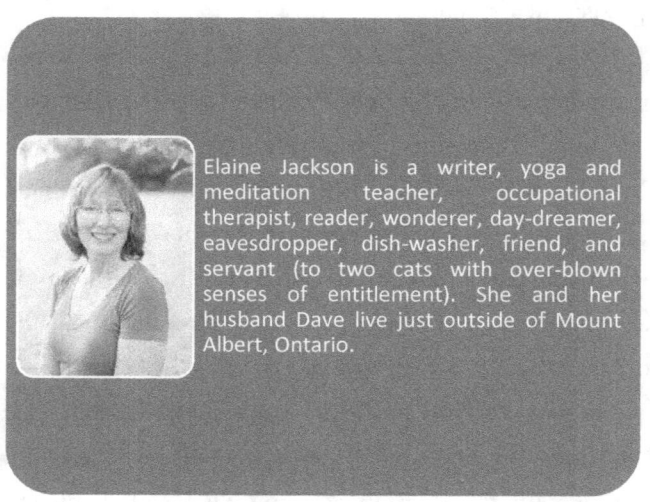

Elaine Jackson is a writer, yoga and meditation teacher, occupational therapist, reader, wonderer, day-dreamer, eavesdropper, dish-washer, friend, and servant (to two cats with over-blown senses of entitlement). She and her husband Dave live just outside of Mount Albert, Ontario.

March of the Androgynous

By E. E. Blake

~1~

N ever in my own lifetime did I think moving back to Shorebrooke was possible. I'd left three years ago, and have been a well-adjusted city girl, ever since.

Not going to lie, Toronto wasn't easy – I was buried beneath two jobs. During the week, I part-timed days at The Condom Shack on Queen Street W, and held a key-holder barista position at the Church-Wellesley Second Cup at night and on the weekends.

Neither job offered any sort of financial security, and barely granted me enough time to volunteer at the 519 Church Street Community Centre. My back pockets were a constant cash-funnel branching off in all different directions, rarely ever looping back to my savings account.

But I did *okay*. I had a roof, food, utilities, and just enough spare to go towards prescriptions and whatever necessities I could find on sale or pre-owned.

Shorebrooke did me no good and Toronto offered a fresh start. Though I lived in poverty limbo, filled with apocalyptic dread each week between paycheques, I remained healthy, independent, and alive. I was pretty lucky for a person in my situation, and despite it all, I was grateful for what I had.

But the day Mom and Dad Skyped me to say that Jay and his wife Marie were expecting their first kid, I knew I had to go back. The chance to mend gaping wounds with estranged people I once loved would not drop out of thin air like this ever again.

Megan Duffy was moving back to Shorebrooke.

I don't remember boarding the 65A Union-New Ansnorveldt GO, but I remember waking up confused to the setting sun's descent behind an endless wall of dense forest, outside my window. The ghost of my panda-toqued reflection stared at me. My hand was vibrating, deep inside my winter coat pocket. During the trip, up until that point, my little Motorola flip-phone fell victim to an anxiety-stricken vice grip.

I withdrew my phone from my jacket pocket. The name *DAD* appeared against the glow of the caller ID.

I answered.

"Sorry to bug you," he said. "Your mom wanted to know if you'd eaten yet."

"Yeah – no – it's okay. Don't worry about me."

"Are you sure, Megs?"

"Yeah, I ate already. At the station."

"Oh. Well. Okay. We'll go ahead without you then. Are you sure?"

Then in my sleepy haze, I realized what was being asked of me. "What are you guys having?"

"Nothing fancy. Matty asked for Sloppy Joes and fries."

"I haven't had Sloppy Joes in forever."

Dad was silent on the other end. For a long while I tried to sit on my apprehension. Finally, he chuckled into my ear. "It'll be good to have you home, Megan. It hasn't been the same – it really hasn't."

The urge to tell Dad I loved him brewed in the pit of my throat. I cleared it away. "Hey, um, do you want me to call you when I pull in?"

"Don't worry about it. I'll there to pick you up at the platform."

"Okay. Hey, Dad – thanks. A lot."

"Thank *you*, Megan. I'll see you in a bit."

~2~

The bus pulled up to the only platform at the New Ansnorveldt GO Station just after 7:00 p.m.. I struggled to contain another anxiety attack under the assault of my own inner demons.

What if Jay *is there tonight?*
What if I run into somebody I used to know?
What if Dad doesn't come?

I got up from my seat and merged with a slow and, ever-awkward, single-file shuffle of folk down the narrow aisle. My eyes scanned the bus windows out into the terminal yard. Tinted, reinforced pane after tinted, reinforced pane only bore the dull, weathered, brown-brick exterior of the station illuminated beneath the glow of eaves-mounted security lights.

Dad was nowhere in sight.

I thanked the driver and took my leave down the steep bus steps. Cold wind blasted my face. Winter was on its way out in Toronto, but here in New Ansnorveldt, the trees and buildings were still war-waged by Mother Nature. Mountain-high snow banks scattered the parking lot as fresh white flakes descended from the clouds, like Vietnam para-troopers.

Other passengers disappeared inside the station or met up with waiting friends or relatives and vanished into the semidarkness of the parking lot.

I got my suitcase from the bus's cargo-bay-thinger and trudged towards the station doors. The large window that saw into the terminal showcased a small group of people inside. Some sat around reading Metro papers or fiddled with their phones. Others chatted idly, while a sparse few sat alone, lost in their own thoughts or observations of the gritty midtown bus-yard.

None of these people resembled the hulking, labour-bodied, Matt Duffy Sr.

I went to the washroom to freshen up.

This whole situation was surreal, out-of-body – like I was watching myself at a distance. But this was happening.

I'm on my way back to Shorebrooke.

No dream. This was real – filmed before a live studio audience.

My reflection over the cracked washroom mirror told the teleplay of a girl whose dark-haired, freckled face exemplified ashen-cheeked terror.

I don't belong here.

I buried my face into my mittens and massaged the flesh around my eyes.

"What are you doing?" I asked. "Life threw you a d20 die and rolled a crit. You landed a natural *20*. Never, ever, in a million years will you get another chance like this! Come on. This is Mom and Dad. This is not a bad situation. They're not the ones who walked away – *you did.*"

But still, poison-tipped thoughts kept jabbing.

I shouldn't be here.

I stuffed my mitts into my coat pocket and splashed cold water on my face to cement the *reality contract.* No more running away. Three years was long enough. I'd changed, and so had Jay. I couldn't write off the countless Skype calls with my folks over the past couple of weeks. Both Mom and Dad were super stoked to have me move back home. They *wanted* me back home – Dad, Mom, Matty.

But really, they weren't why I left, to begin with.

~3~

I spotted him as soon as I exited the washroom.

He sat with his back to me on one of four benches between a large, murky-glassed schedule directory. His alabaster baldness adorned a mite of crown stubble. His wide shoulders heaved beneath that worn-out emerald spring coat Mom hated, but he wore everywhere anyway – easily recognizable in any sea of balding, ill-fashioned, fathers.

Dad's arm stretched across the metal backrest. He gazed pensively from side to side, to the dark window that saw out into platform and the distant parking lot. I wasn't the only one nervous.

I trotted up behind him with my suitcase wheeling at my heels. I reached across the empty bench behind his, and placed a gentle hand on his shoulder.

He looked up at me with warm, sleepy eyes, his signature teeny-tiny perma-smile that rarely faded.

"Hey," I said.

"Hiya." Dad rose to his feet and took a good look at me. Somehow I'd forgotten how tall he was. At six-foot-a-million, he easily towered over my squeaky five-four-nothing.

I blushed and looked down at the bench that separated us.

"Nice ears." Dad gently tugged one of the panda ears on my toque.

"Don't do that," I said with an apprehensive laugh. My eyes flicked up to see his smile grow.

"You look real good, Megs," Dad said.

My nervous smile broadened into a soft grin. "You too."

Dad opened his mouth like he wanted to say something else, but he didn't — at least, not right away. He looked off towards the parking lot, then back to me. "Well, I guess we should get out of here, huh? Those Sloppy Joes aren't gonna eat 'emselves."

"Yeah"

"This all you have?" Dad asked in mid-reach for my suitcase.

"Yeah," I said with a half-embarrassed chuckle. I passed it off to him and cleared my throat. "That's all she wrote."

Dad smiled at me again. "It's good to see you, Megan. Good to have you home."

~4~

The twenty-minute drive back to Mom and Dad's place in Shorebrooke started out pretty quiet I couldn't help but reflect back on Uma Thurman's rant on uncomfortable silence from *Pulp Fiction*. I expected a dreadfully awkward ride home, but there was no discomfort. Our silence during the ride back was strangely *natural*, despite our time away from each other. Two people simply enjoying each other's company, just as Uma Thurman described *comfortable silence* should be.

After awhile, Dad spoke, "Can I drop an elephant in the back seat?"

I turned my head from the passenger window to look at him.

"Whatever happened between you and Jay is between you and Jay ..." – He took a breath – "... but I want you to know that your mother and I love and support you no matter what. We might not fully *understand* what you're going through or why you *chose* to do what ... you did – but you're our child, and we *love* you."

It felt good to hear Dad say that. He and Mom had said it a few times before, when we'd talked on Skype, but to hear the words face-to-face ...

"You told him I'm moving back in?"

"He called last week about borrowing the van and my work ladder for a dump run. Did we tell you he's putting in an addition?"

"The new nursery for Bella, right? What did he say?"

Dad didn't answer.

"Is he gonna be there tonight?"

"Nope," he said, enunciating the p with a pop.

"That's too bad," I muttered, and scratched a familiar itch on one of my wrists. I looked back out the window. If my brother didn't wish to initiate, it was clear my pawn had the first move. I reached into my coat pocket and withdrew a folded piece of scrap paper.

"What's that?"

"Just Jay's number. Mom gave it to me last time we talked, but I haven't had the guts to call him." I sighed and put the piece of paper back in my pocket.

Dad placed a big, rugged hand on my knee and gave it a supportive squeeze. For a tough dude who worked hellish shifts at a lumberyard, alongside small-town hetero-alcoholics, it always fascinated me just how soft and warm he was - despite his gritty, chap-skinned exterior. I took his hand and gave it a gentle squeeze back.

We exited off of Highway 11 between New Ansnorveldt and Shorebrooke's cramped upper-town, and rounded a short bridge that showcased the "scenic" parts of the marsh in all its blistery, wintry, glory. Home was just around the bend. We passed a sign that read "ROUGH ROAD AHEAD."

I remember thinking: *You got that right, dude.*

~5~

Dad closed the door behind me, "We're home!"

I could hear the hiss of pulled pork cooking on the pan. The smell of barbeque sauce was intoxicating. From the kitchen, Mom yelped gleeful reunion. This roused Matty; I heard him peel rubber against the hardwood floor from somewhere down the hall. Mom appeared and pulled me into a bear-hug. Before I could regain any sense of balance, I felt my little brother's arms tight around my waist, his cheek planted against my hip.

I shot a look of helplessness to Dad. He offered a wry smirk and shrugged at me, then disappeared downstairs with my luggage.

"Megan, is that all you brought with you?" Mom balked as Dad passed by us.

I blushed. "Yeah."

Mom waved the air apologetically and hugged me once more.

"It's so good to see you," she whispered in my ear, now on the verge of tears. Matty was heavy around my waist. I pulled them both closer. Tears welled up behind my closed eyes, but I held them back.

"You too," I said.

Our group hug lasted for an eternity. The smell of dinner brought on a strange sensation in the pit of my stomach. Nostalgia over-rode my senses. Yes, the smell of Sloppy Joes brought on a whole influx of emotions, memories. Great memories; memories that involved these perfect, perfect, strangers.

One memory in particular opened up to me, fresh and vivid like a newly-installed window frame. About five or six months before I left – we were sitting around the kitchen table on a Wednesday night …

"So, Matty was sent home from school today," Mom had casually announced as she passed a bowl of mashed potatoes to Dad.

Immediately, my interest piqued. "What'd he do this time?"

Mom cleared her throat. "Mr. Quinn told me he slipped out a little saying today at recess. I believe the exact words were, 'I'm off like a prom-dress.'"

"*Nice!*" I exclaimed and wheeled around in my seat to face Matty, who had slunk into his spot at the table. He looked like a fearful soldier seeking refuge from flying shrapnel. "Tell me they gave you a Leacock for that one!"

I didn't see the corner of Dad's mouth ticking, but my Spidey-senses tingled.

"Apparently," Mom stated, "someone else in this household enjoys a similar phrase …" Her eyes darted up from her plate and locked on mine.

Check and mate.

"Welp, thanks for dinner, guys!" I said and rushed towards the hallway portal. "I'm stuffed!"

"Hold your daisies, *Pronto*saurus Rex." Dad pointed to my empty seat. "Sit back down ..."

The memory faded, and I was left in the embrace of my family. Mom pulled away with reluctance. She held me at shoulder's length and examined my body up and down with puffy eyes and a pursed smile upon her face. "You've changed so much."

"Yeah," was all I could say. I smiled at her, patted Matty on his little head. I *had* changed.

~6~

Mom and Matty took me downstairs and showed me to my old room. Dad was just heading out into the basement hallway when we met on the landing. He stepped away and led everybody back inside.

We entered a museum exhibit entitled *Relics of a Lost Duffy:* wood-panelled walls were covered with an eclectic collection of movie and music posters – favourites being the *I Spit on Your Grave* wall mural above my closet door that Mom hated so much, and my coveted Sonic Youth LIVE (with Nirvana and STP) at the Hollywood Palladium poster that hung across from my window. Bookcases and hanging shelves were crammed with various paperbacks and movies. An oak vanity stood cluttered with makeup and stuffed animals. On my desk sat an old thirteen-inch TV, CD player, clear-cased telephone, and a Sega Genesis with *Sonic the*

97

Hedgehog 2 still popped into the cartridge deck. My bed stuck out into the middle of the room, its lime-coloured blanket neatly made and the pillows freshly-cased and puffed up against the headboard.

Easter dinner, three years ago, I'd stormed out of the house in tears, a backpack over my shoulder stuffed with just clothes and money. The last I saw of my bedroom, it'd been a state not unlike a ransacked crime scene left by Richard Ramirez, *the Night Stalker.*

But bless her heart, Mom cleaned the place up like I'd never left.

"Come on," Dad said to Mom and Matty. I felt Mom's hand slip from my shoulder. My family left me standing in the time capsule of my old bedroom.

I took a minute to absorb the atmosphere. I threw my panda toque onto the vanity and tossed my coat onto the bed. I tugged out my small ponytail and scruffed at the back of my head to make my dark hair fall into its natural bobbed state.

I took my time unpacking and reordered my room around to fit the few cherished things from my apartment – knick-knacks mostly: a tiny ceramic cat statue from Kensington Market, framed photos of friends from my volunteer gig at the 519, a couple of hard-to-find horror movies from Bay Video – sentimental things I couldn't bring myself to pitch or pawn off for cash when I decided to come back.

I rooted around in my jacket for my phone, but only

found my mittens, crumpled up receipts, and candy bar wrappers. Everything except for my mitts went into the trash. I hung my coat up on a hook behind the door and sat down on the bed.

A long and heavy breath escaped my lungs. I gazed around. There were so many memories, so much time spent in this bedroom, this *house*. This was where I grew up. Before Toronto, I knew nothing else. I leaned back on my arms and closed my eyes to the last time I was here …

How could you do such a stupid thing? Do Mom and Dad know? What about Matty? He's just a kid, for Christ's sake! How's he supposed to understand? Who are you? What are you?

A shiver sent me upright at the foot of my bed. It'd happened so long ago, but Jay's words ripped and twisted like a fresh razor across my flesh. I massaged my right wrist and went over to the desk.

I patted around for the slip of paper with his number on it, but all my hands felt were my butt and my misplaced Motorola. I searched my front pockets. Nothing. Anxiety clawed up my throat. My eyes found my jacket. I pounced. Those pockets were empty, too.

The trash bin.

I floundered back across the room, grabbed the wire-basket by the rim and dumped the contents on the floor. My searching fingers raked through candy bar wrappers, crumpled receipts, used Kleenexes, and makeup-stained wipes and wedges. I combed through the trash a second time until black-inked numbers stared up at me through a fold in a small sheet of paper. I snatched it up.

This whole situation wouldn't fester any longer. The maggots had brewed in the mounds of family decay for long enough. I went to the desk, yanked the clear-cased receiver off its cradle, and punched in Jay's number. The line rang.

Another panic attack stiffened my muscles. I rooted myself into my swivel chair to quell the strong urge to hang up.

On the sixth ring, the line connected.

"Hi, you've reached Jason and Marie Duffy. Leave a message at the tone."

Beeeeeeeeep.

I straightened against the backrest and cleared my throat.

"Uh ... hi, Jay. It's—" I paused, bowed my chin. Closed my eyes and shook my head. "It's Megan – your *sister*," I rebounded with a firm tone. "I'm at Mom and Dad's. Please give me a shout when you get in ... I'd really love to talk."

I paused again.

"Congratulations on the new baby ... I love you. Bye."

I sighed and hung up. The Leafs would win the play-offs before Jay would ever call back. But the important thing was that I had at least done my part – I *tried*.

~7~

I went upstairs to see if Mom needed help with anything in the kitchen. She was fine, and sent me away to go "make myself at home." I didn't want to bother Matty while he did homework at the kitchen table, and Dad was in the den reading that day's paper with Coach's Corner blaring in the background.

I ended up in the family room. Scratching away at another itch on one of my wrists, I trudged over to the bay window. It was pretty crappy out. The sky was pitch black and snow rained down in a thin veil. Tree branches flailed all helpless in the night's wind.

I folded my arms against the sill and nuzzled my cheek against the crooks of my elbows before squinting out into the street. Across the road, Mrs. Petrovich's war-time bungalow stared me down with its two darkened, hateful front windows.

A small break formed in the clouds, where the crescent moon peeked through.

"Goodnight, Moon," I murmured.

It was the middle of March. March meant the coming of spring, and spring meant the coming of growth and rejuvenation; preparation for the summer. Maybe it was a sign.

Everything was going to be okay.

God, I sure hope so.

I pushed away from the window and found myself gazing at a collection of framed pictures set up on the fireplace mantle. Mom was a professional home-stager. All of the photos were set up in an attractive style that rivalled old 1990s Hallmark commercials. Each picture with its own frame, but somehow none of it clashed with the living room décor, each angled just perfectly.

My eyes glossed over photo after photo that spanned years and years of the Duffy family history. The first held an image of Dad at the kitchen table, blowing out the candles at his 45th birthday, seven years ago. It was the first and last time I ever saw him wear a coned celebratory hat, and I'm sure it was only to humour Mom.

The second picture: a six-year-old Jay outside our garage, squinting into the camera on a bright 1987 July afternoon, while balanced on the training wheels of his brand-new bike. He'd been in the hospital for something, I'd forgotten what, and Mom and Dad got him the bike as a recovery gift – next, Mom and Dad's wedding photo outside of St. Augustine's in Mapleton, thirty-three years ago. October 21st, 1982. God, they were so young – then, a picture I took of Matty a few years ago. He was seven then, cuddled up on the couch beneath a blanket, smiling into the camera, cheek-to-cheek with our late orange tabby, Ravioli. My eyes skipped to the next photo. The blood in my cheeks turned to ice.

High school graduation.

Discomfort settled on my shoulders as I examined the short, tidy hair, the shadow of shaved facial stubble. A forced smile. Superficial eyes that hid sadness and contempt, a teenager lost in self-destructive depression. I didn't know who this person was anymore, a total stranger to me now. *Kevin Duffy* – a mind sealed within a body not meant to co-exist.

The long-since healed razorblade scars up both my wrists reminded me of that every single day.

I felt a pair of hands caress my shoulders from behind with gentle affection.

"I like your hair like this," Mom whispered to me. I thought at first she meant the picture, but then she brushed some strands of my current do behind one ear. "Did you see the newest one?"

I looked over to the opposite end of the mantle and fell into further shock. Encased in a brown, formal wood-frame stood a self-shot I took at Percé Rock, while on vacation two years ago in Quebec.

In the photo I wore a bright, genuine smile. My eyes were wide, round, and filled with true happiness. Longer hair, slightly-kinked by misty wind, gusted in the cool beach air. That photo encapsulated who I truly was – authentic to myself, for the first time. Free, like the seagulls around me.

"I hope you don't mind," Mom said, "I scooped it off of your Facebook."

I turned and caught her smiling down at me. She enveloped my body into her familiar, loving embrace.

And then everything hit me. Everything with Jay, and coming back to Shorebrooke – all of my fears and worries simply washed away. Here – *home* – was right where I needed to be. This was where I belonged. The obvious had been screaming at me from behind, even from the start of my transition.

Whatever happened with Jay and me was in the past. Nothing could be rewritten, but the future still held hope, as dim as that hope's glimmer was. The new chance life had given me was this: it was time to move on and surround myself with those who *wanted* to be present, no matter what – those who'd been my biggest supporters from birth.

"I love you so much, Megan," Mom whispered in my ear.

"I love you too, Mom." The tears I held back earlier took fruition once more. "I'm sorry – I'm so sorry I hurt us."

Mom squeezed me closer to her body.

"Shh … you're here now. I love you so much." She started to rock me in her arms, like when I was younger. "Welcome home, baby. Welcome home."

In that moment, still absorbing the revelation, all of my walls crumbled.

I held her close to me and let my tears fall.

E.E. Blake is a Young Adult indie author with backgrounds in journalism, psychology, and pop-culture analysis - E.E. encourages readers to connect via Twitter and Wattpad @EEBlake.

Army Invisible
By Paul Telegdi

A vengeful wind blasted into the recessed angle of the building and swooped down on the prone form bundled on the pavement against the bitter cold. The rumpled heap shivered, curling into a ball, to conserve heat. The turbulence receded, but it would return.

Should he move to a better protected spot? A small vent from the building's maintenance room exhaled some warmth, so he pressed closer to better absorb the flow before the night claimed it all. It was too late, he decided, to move now and risk exposing himself to the bite of the wind racing down Dundas Street. Besides, this was a good spot - public enough so the Mission Truck could find him again. They knew where he was, having dropped off a sleeping bag for him to use earlier. With a warning about the declared cold alert, they had tried to convince him to go to their hospice. He'd been tempted, but had scored a bottle of wine and didn't want it confiscated. No, he'd tough it out with his bottle: the 25 percent alcohol his antifreeze. The Mission people promised to be back around four AM to bring him something hot.

God, it was cold! By far the coldest night this winter. What did the Mission Man say, minus 25 with wind chill? Under the covers he shrugged. What did it matter? Minus

25 or minus 30 even. After a certain point, it no longer made any appreciable difference. They, with their thermometers, differentiating the temperature into convenient degrees, what did they really know of the cold? The cold that radiated from the ground, that permeated his very soul.

His body felt lethargic with the all-pervasive distress of his separate parts. They should be hurting more, he reasoned. Worried, he wiggled his toes hard against the insides of his boots until the feeling of pain returned. Thank God he had the fleece-lined boots he'd traded with another homeless for cigarettes, a bottle, and some change. Otherwise, on a night like this, he could lose his toes to frostbite like Turncoat Tommy, who hung around Grosvenor Square, modeling his reversible coat that he sardonically described as casual outer wear with a darker inside for more formal occasions.

What time was it? Two AM? God, let it be closer to daybreak. He dared not sleep; afraid to never wake again, he clutched the sleeping bag close. He had on his parka and two shirts underneath, but the chill still penetrated the layers. Having stuffed newspapers into the linings, the Star, the Post, the Mail, for extra insulation he combatted the weather any way possible.

"You're finally in the news, buddy," he muttered to himself, but the words incited a fit of coughing that awoke every complaint in his body. It hurt again, but that was a good sign - as long as he hurt, his limbs and organs were functioning. Pain was the last process to surrender before death. He shivered as the chill wormed its way into his mind, congealing his thoughts.

Footsteps approached. This late? The bars were long closed. Please God, don't let it be the thugs who rolled him three nights ago, kicking him in the ribs. And for what? Two dollars in change? They were looking for weed they said. As if he had any.

The steps paused inside his private space, and he tensed.

"Are you all right?" a good Samaritan asked.

"Buzz off," he hissed. It was too cold to beg or suffer fools. Did he look all right? The feet went away.

He pushed his face into the fleece of the sleeping bag, inhaling the warmth of his own breath, anxious to retain the heat. He sniffed the fabric, likely a donation at the public call for aid to the homeless. A smell of normalcy still lingered. When was it last used? The previous summer, on a family camping trip?

Once he too had a name, a home, a family. He was Mr. Robinson of 132 Woodhaven, Etobicoke. Had a regular nine-to-five job that often extended into overtime, and a late model luxury car in the driveway of an upscale property. He had bank accounts, a credit rating, and several club memberships. Now it was all gone. His papers stolen in a downtown hospice, his identity expired. How did it come to this?

Thousands of stories littered the street, but only a few basic paths to ruin: addiction, bankruptcy, mental illness, abuse and abandonment ... all leading to loss of roots and purpose. For him it had been alcohol; a drink for lunch, a few after work, beers in front of the TV, and a night-cap. After years of neglect, the wife divorced him. She found a new life in Scarborough and he hadn't seen the children in three years. He could barely recall their faces any more. If she were smart, she'd tell them he was dead and done.

There was more alcohol after that, and more reasons to drink. He lost his job, his place, then everything else. He bounced around between friends and relatives, who tried to save him, but after eight months they turned him out. He tried to sober up then, undergoing detox and rehab, but in a moment of weakness alcohol claimed him again.

He became Slim Jim on account of his narrow frame, one of the overlooked of the Army of the Invisible that lived on the underside of Toronto. He shared the streets with the dispossessed, the burnt-out derelicts, the lost, the naive, and the runaways – where many teens sold their youth on the sidewalk. At least they had something to sell.

Not far back he'd tried to get a job, pretending to be middle-class, but his eyes shone and gave away the truth his lies could not cover. His rumpled, lived-in clothes told on him. And there was a rancid smell. How was he even to afford the fare for an interview? There had been the occasional washing of dishes, delivering of flyers, sweeping a parking lot, or worse, snow shovelling.

Panhandling was his real job now. On the corner of Dundas and Lansdowne, where he staked out a claim and defended it against his kind, like the half-cripple Viet Rob who'd been eyeing the intersection. On a good morning, five dollars in coins would collect in his hat.

"Please, can you spare some change?" he'd intone in a weary monotone. But there was a mandatory protocol to be observed: don't ever look directly at them; they pay you not to capture their eyes; don't dare to flaunt your invisibility; they pay the ransom to pass you by unseen.

He shivered, clutching his folded arms closer, peering into the sky. In the crisp, bitter cold, halos surrounded every light. God, please, let it be near morning. A street car rattled by, the wheels screeching on the cold rails and a shower of sparks cascaded from the transmission wires overhead. Five o'clock then, three more hours yet to go.

His teeth chattered. He took a quick swig of the wine, nesting the bottle back on his chest protectively. It was so goddamn cold! Quick, think of something else.

Someone said once that we were all just four paycheques from bankruptcy, and maybe only six from the streets. With him, it was more the number of drinks that got him here. In seventeen years of indulging, he'd imbibed what? 70,000 maybe 90,000 drinks? God! Where was all that lovely alcohol? Now the bottle was his mother, his wife, friend and … enemy. It left him time for little else.

Had he wasted his life entirely? Made so little of it? In the good old days, it was the comfort of routines that stole his time from what really mattered: to take care of his relationships. Life on the street was made long by the lack of purpose, except for indulging in self-pity. But now he was beyond shame, free of guilt, all blame paid for by his depravations. He no longer dwelled on a past that had happened to someone else; not to Slim Jim, who had no future and no longer bothered to look beyond tomorrow. He had no regrets, his bottle took care of that. Was survival not enough?

They want to count us, he thought with rare derision. The City needed exact figures to debate, to massage the statistics and congratulate themselves that the percentages were in decline. A shell game. Now you see us and now you don't, the Army of the Invisible. Will they open more shelters? With more rules and bureaucracy? No alcohol! No drugs! No sex! No lice! No humanity! There was instead intimidation and fear. Wait until I get you on the outside!

The shelters and refuges were pressure cookers. Rows of cots: in the next a wino confessing his delirium and further down a derelict coughing up his lungs, spreading his disease - how was one supposed to sleep? Don't the people who run these places know what's happening in them? No wonder the lost-people stayed away. On the street at least, in spite of the fear and violence, remained a desperate sort of freedom; free to starve and die without having to be accountable.

A truck rumbled by, the vibration reaching the prone figure, rousing his aches. A dog came around the building, intruding on the man's privacy, sniffed twice then backed away not liking the smell. Running feet passed, bringing fresh anxiety.

Slim Jim shut his mind to the outside. Sure, there were a few good people who championed the cause of the dispossessed. They provided aid and comfort to the helpless, for they were do-gooders. But did they not know how irritating they were, smugly brandishing their good deeds? People without hope have long lost the capacity for respect and gratitude. Couldn't they understand a simple thing like that? The fact of it was that the street was a hustle, the clock around. Everybody wanted something from them. The authorities wanted to clean up Toronto – homelessness was not good for tourism. There were the predators that preyed on the unprotected, exploiting their weaknesses. Even the charities were harassing to rescue the dispossessed. And the churches needed their quota of souls.

One day they would discover his body in some godforsaken hole and would make a cause of him, write him up in the papers trying to give substance to a sad statistic. How could it happen in our fair city? The truth was, that while he lived, no one cared.

Don't sleep. Don't close your eyes. Don't let your mind fool you that you're in a warm bed, or you won't ever wake again. Would that be such a bad thing? To give himself a jolt he thought of sex. When was the last time? On a bitter cold night, like this, a prostitute took pity and invited him to her place. She let him have a bath – he remembered that.

Must have been three, four years ago. No! That couldn't be right. Four years ago he was still trying to be normal.

Yet if the nights were long, the days were even longer, filled with walking. Constantly walking to keep the Invisibility on the move. Past windows of displays he could not afford; past fast food places reeking of meals he could not pay for; past grocery stores with their bins full of exotic produce, with the owners glowering at him. Everywhere sights of excess and luxury, in which he had no share. Move on, invite no attention, give them no reason to call the cops. The jails were worse than the shelters – overcrowded cells with urine and vomit on the floor. No thanks. Move on, pause in a doorway just long enough to catch a gust of warmth, move on again. Piecemeal loitering, just long enough to find energy for the next little bit.

Was it Tuesday today or Thursday? It was December twenty something ... God, had he missed Christmas? No – they would have served turkey at the Mission, he would have remembered that. After that they'd coax them into singing those damn carols. For Christmas he would like ... an unopened bottle of scotch, the seal still gloriously intact ... and maybe a corned beef sandwich from the deli to go with it.

Stan, the Mission Truck driver, shook him awake. Helping Slim Jim to sit up, he pressed a Styrofoam cup into his hands.

"Drink some of this, old timer."

Old? He was only thirty-seven, younger than the driver.

"Come with us to the shelter," Stan invited in a carefully neutral tone. Don't push now, the quarry might bolt. Slim concentrated on the heat in his hands, the taste slowly thawing on his taste buds. Chocolate.

Should he, shouldn't he? He'd fallen asleep. If it were not for the Mission Truck … well then? On the other hand, the worst was over now, and there were still two fingers of his life left in the bottle. Risk that and face the critical appraisal at the shelter, the intake questions that tired him so? Face the humid, seedy smell of the room filled with unwashed clothes? He shuddered. The cold, at least, did not smell.

"No," he mumbled, holding out the cup for refill. Stan shrugged. The truck rumbled off, trolling for more of the hopeless, maybe more amenable.

A little later, a bus crossed the intersection belching a cloud of diesel fumes into his refuge and reluctantly he stirred, unbending each joint, and straightened with the weight of the night heavy on him. He took a step toward his corner on Dundas and Lansdowne.

Frenchy was in the wind-shadow of the kiosk near the subway, trying to breathe life into his fingers. His eyes were bleary from the cheap drink the night before.

"I see you made it," he observed.

"Yeah. Survived one more night." But for how long?

Slim Jim offered a butt and they huddled sharing its comfort. Later, they ambled off toward the park where on a least bit sunny day, they'd meet the rest, huddled together like penguins, taking comfort in their own small numbers. Yes, there was Crackhead Sue, Indian Jill with her four-year-old son, Buzz, handicapped Anthony who chose the streets instead of the home catering to his special needs, and there was Slim Jim, who belonged to no one now, and owed allegiance to none, not even to the Army of the Invisible.

Paul Telegdi is a self-published author of 23 books and is still writing. He's proud to be married to his long-time sweetheart and has three grown sons.

The Finalities of Cecil and Sylvie

By Nancy Thorne

T he walk up the hill felt longer with each new spring, but of course she realized the hill was not the one changing.

Despite yesterday's rain, the patch of grass beneath the dense umbrella of the grand maple was parched and yellow. Sylvie spread the blanket over the scraggy indentations of the soil and carefully lowered herself until she felt comfortable: knees bent to the side, rested on one buttock, anchored by an outstretched arm at her side.

"The irony of this whole thing, Cecil," she said as a wisp of wind lifted the fringe of her hair, "is that you just needed to wait a bit longer and everything would have turned out just like you wanted." She looked up to the sound of rustling leaves followed by hungry quick chirps from a bird's nest and concentrated on that for a moment.

"I mean, don't you remember you were always that way? You wanted what you wanted when you wanted it. And mostly, you ended up with exactly whatever it was you wanted." Sylvie kept her attention focused on the upper limbs until she recognized the plump red breast of a robin as it darted from between the branches in search of another worm.

"I grant that you always were the intelligent one, Cecil. I always knew I was the one relegated to loving you more than I loved myself. But I never slighted you for it, you have to admit." She nodded a couple of times in this acknowledgement.

"When we were teenagers you wanted to play the guitar, remember that? Next thing I know, there you are just playing and singing your fool head off. I've got to hand it to you, Cecil. You were pretty damn good."

She looked out to the vastness of the landscape and caught a glimpse of the few people sauntering among the maze of trunks.

"And remember the day you told me you wanted to be a doctor? Well, I knew better than to place any doubt on that one."

Sylvie slowly stood and braced her feet against the uneven terrain before she placed her hands on her hips and looked over the ground as if in search of a worm for herself.

"But I wouldn't be honest if I didn't tell you, Cecil, that I was almost ready to do myself in when you told me that you no longer wanted *me*. Oh yes, I know you've heard this a thousand times before, but I'm still trying to get my head around it. Tossed aside like a worn out shoe is how it felt at the time, I want to tell you."

A young man with dark curls that swirled above his eyebrows caught Sylvie's eye just as she finished a stroll around the girth of the tree. He stood at the edge of the roadway, still and alone. She knew it couldn't be an acquaintance; no one knew where she was. She stretched her body from side to side before sinking back onto the blanket.

"Where was I was then. Oh yes. Well, what was I to do? Maybe you would have seen right through him if you'd met him, Cecil. Maybe you could have warned me. But timing is everything, just like they say, I guess. And we both know that your timing was as bad as it could possibly be."

She glanced again at the young man who had not moved from the spot where she had first noticed him. She wished he had a blanket of his own so he could relax for a while atop the slight damp of the emerald grass that flourished just ahead of where he stood.

"I may have mentioned to you last year when I came to visit that I in no way resent the years I spent working for us as a store clerk; all those years you were in medical school. But the honest-to-goodness truth is I don't even know what the truth is anymore. All I can tell you is that the day I remarried I felt pretty smug. I had moved on, Cecil. Even when I heard you were in graduate school to become a cardiologist I barely blinked an eye. Not so much as even one of the people around me would have noticed any change in my demeanor. I only smiled with my teeth showing, just the way you always said you liked."

Sylvie let her body drift and unfurl over the blanket, then felt the back of her head come in contact with a mound of soil. She settled into it as if it were a firm pillow and tilted her face to one side – the young man was still waiting, still silent.

She created scenarios for him in her mind: he was meeting a friend - a boorish, belated friend that he would admonish at first sight; he was on a dangerous mission as an undercover agent, complete with a shirt-button sized camera that documented everything from his chest as he moved imperceptibly; he had lost a beloved pet and wished for it to appear within his sight somewhere above the expanse of the property; he was simply enjoying the sunshine, the breeze and the solitude, right along with her. She pointed a finger over the satin trim of the blanket.

"And you! Well, of course everyone assumed you were happy. You were getting just what they thought you wanted." She looked up at the sun from her shadowed viewpoint. The sky was clear except for one cloud that hovered above her like a dirigible. She watched as it gradually morphed into the shape of a ragged-edged heart. "A heart. Isn't that just what it looks like Cecil? A subject you know better than most, I suppose… afflictions and such."

It was surprising how comfortable she felt with just the thin weave of the cotton- blend fabric underneath the contours of her body. She would almost swear the land was ever so gradually molding itself around the outline of her head, torso, arms and legs.

"And I must not forget to tell you about the day your letter arrived. I know it's not your favourite part of the story, but of course I can't just let it go unmentioned." She tapped her fingers on top of the blanket.

"Well, the day your letter arrived, I was painting the baby's room. I cried when I read it. Do you remember me telling you that, Cecil? I cried because I was so happy you wanted me back. I cried because I realized you hadn't heard

I was a wife and mother. I cried because I knew you would be in pain, not getting what you wanted and all."

Sylvie glanced again at the young man who had started to walk up the hill. She wished she had brought her eyeglasses along. It would be nice to get a better look at him.

"Of course I'm sure you agree that I had no other option than to let you know about my newborn son. The thing of it is, Cecil, from the moment he came into my life, I could only see ahead. And I felt sorry for you then; sorry you could only see behind." She took a hand and swiped away the blades of grass that had hitched with a gust and settled on the engraved three and five of the granite headstone that lay level beside her head.

"How could it have come to this," she muttered to herself, knowing. "All you had to do was wait a few years."

The young man seemed to be moving in a straight line toward Sylvie. She wanted to sit up and look around to see exactly who else was in the immediate vicinity he may be headed for, but was just too comfortable to move. Melodic whistles drifted into her ears. A tranquil balmy current enfolded her skin as if she had dipped into a warm bath. She closed her eyes and continued.

"I always thought it would be me, the one who ceased to be." She brought her hand to her mouth to stifle a laugh. "Listen to me, Cecil. Bet you didn't know you are in love with a poet."

The young man stood straight above her and blocked the sun, but she felt no fear. He bent over and offered to guide her to her feet. And as she raised her arms and placed her palms into his, she couldn't help but notice the smooth, porcelain skin of her hands and the youthfulness of her straight fingers. She looked up into his eyes. "Cecil," she said.

The young man gazed at Sylvie with all the want she had deftly visualized during private moments over the past four decades. "I've been waiting a long time for you Sylvie," he said.

"I figured you would be," said Sylvie.

Nancy Thorne began her lifelong goal of becoming a writer in 2011 after retiring to the town of Whitby with her husband, two sons and a yellow lab.

The Chase ~ *a true story*

By Joanna Gale

First of all, keep in mind this was my lunch hour, the air a-jingle with its Christmas bustle under a cloudy sky just waiting to sprinkle her white stuff all over. And, I was taking full advantage of checking some gifts off my long list in a few favourite shops of mine along The Bloor West Village.

Time was up. My lunch hour over, I needed to get back to work. I hurried to the parking lot, set some of the parcels that were jam-packing my arms on the roof of my car, and unlocked the door. Tossing the parcels in the back, I quickly got myself in the front, and flew up Windermere Avenue to Annette Street where I stopped at my turn.

And, that's where it all began.

A dark car on Annette Street, heading in the same direction, had stopped to the right of me, allowing a pedestrian with her shopping buggy to cross the intersection. *Good.* This opened the way for me to make a quick left onto Annette Street. However, almost immediately after I'd turned, I heard the loud, constant honking of a car horn. *Where was that coming from and why? Was a pedestrian about to walk into my path? Had I cut someone off.* I quickly searched all directions. *Nothing.*

Through my rear-view mirror I saw that same dark car on my back bumper — lights flashing, horn beeping, and the male driver flailing his arms and head madly about — obviously at me. Sometimes he'd swing his arm out the window, gesturing for me to pull over, but I forged ahead determined not to let him get the best of me. *What is his problem? Darn men, always on about women drivers.* I mean, he was after me, acting as if I'd cut him off or done something illegal. I hadn't done anything wrong. He was stopped. I had the right of way, and my signal was on and working. *No way am I stopping for this crazy man. I don't have time for this.*

But the man persisted with his frantic waving, frequently motioning me over to the curb. Thank goodness Jane Street was close enough for me to make the green light. *Now he'd give up the chase and turn the other way.* Well, not exactly.

As I neared the corner and veered into the right lane, he sped up beside me, a crazed look on his face again, frantically gesturing with his right arm while he mouthed something I couldn't hear. Then instead of turning left, he whipped around and with extra speed forced me to stop up against the curb as I turned the corner. *Oh dear, Joanna, this is really serious.* I slumped low in my seat while he pulled a bit farther ahead before braking completely. At the same time, another car pulled into park behind me; the next thing I knew, a woman knocked on my window. *Maybe he's a cop and she was called in as backup? What's going on? A kidnapping, maybe? A theft? A case of mistaken identity? Don't be so silly.*

The woman, now peering through my half-lowered window said, "Ma'am, that gentleman,"—she pointed to the man now relaxed in the dark car—"was trying to get you to stop so you could retrieve your purse."

"My purse?"

"Yes. It flew off the roof of your car back at Windermere Ave. I can't be certain but I think a lady with a red coat may have picked it up and headed for Mary's Hair Salon."

"Thank you," I said, sitting bolt upright and shoving the car into drive, my entire face flushing with embarrassment. I sped off with barely enough time to toss a sheepish wave to the gentleman in the dark car; the man who'd gone above and beyond on my behalf; the man who I'd thought so poorly of, and now had to race past in order to search for my purse.

It wasn't long before I was back at the corner where the mishap had occurred, my heart racing faster than the car. *How foolish. My life is in that purse.*

As I neared Windermere I scanned the street for anyone with an extra purse, or wearing a red jacket. *There she was* — a woman wearing a long, dark-red coat. *Has to be her.* I pulled over.

"Excuse me," I asked. "Have you found a black purse

or seen anyone who may have?"

"No, I'm sorry, but I haven't seen anything."

"Okay. Thank you. Merry Christmas."

By now most of the witnesses would have left the scene. My heart began to sink, even though I was still hopeful that Mary's Hair Salon might, just might, bring my bag back to me.

I parked the car and went into the Salon. No luck. I needed to call work, but I had no money, no license, no identification. So, I headed for home. On the way, I noticed a blonde woman in a red car behind me. She followed me all the way down the hill into our valley off Jane Street. *Wouldn't it be crazy if she has my purse? That's plain silly, too much of a long shot ... it was a* red coat, *not a* red car. *Just get yourself home, Joanna.* Still the possibility niggled at me all the way into the house.

Once inside, I called my supervisor and explained what happened. To my surprise, through all of this commotion it seemed everything was in my favour, as even she told me not to worry about getting back to work, but to concentrate on getting my purse. I hung up and within seconds the phone rang.

"Are you ...?"

"Yes."

"And, do you live at ...?"

"Yes."

"Well, I think I have your purse, but before we go any further, if you could identify the colour and contents of your wallet, date of birth, and a bit more verification that you *are* the rightful owner, you'll have it returned sooner than you think. If I'm correct, we're practically neighbours."

In no time at all I was parked in a driveway behind a red car, standing in front of the same blonde woman who had followed me into the Valley. She graciously handed me my purse, encouraging me to check its contents, which were complete with all my belongings. I grasped her extended hand in both of mine and gazed into the true blue depth of her eyes as I thanked her. Then I rushed home and I sank into the sofa, clutching my handbag.

I've never been able to thank the man who chased me a good couple of blocks before I gave in to his persistence. I doubt he knows how grateful I remain to this day, and he'll never know how foolish I felt after the incident was over. So many people all doing what was right for a complete stranger — the perfect gift — the basic goodness of humanity, along with my purse. Of course.

Joanna Gale has been published in newsletters, chapbooks, anthologies, magazines and other periodicals, as well as on-line. She is a retired Registered Nurse, who currently lives in Markham, Ontario, with her husband.

Junior CSI
By Nanci M. Pattenden

Ted's suggestion to give our son a forensics kit for Christmas was a great idea, or so I thought. I had no inkling how drastically that one gift would change all our lives, yours included. The first few days after Christmas I was constantly wiping black powder off pretty much everything in the house. Sean would powder this, and powder that, looking for anything he thought might be a valued print. He even tried to dust the dog; a rather ugly mix – part Chihuahua, part God only knows what. I'm sure you've seen the beast by now. I suppose he figured it had no hair so it must have prints, right? After a couple of days, the novelty wore off - for me, not Sean.

Naturally he had to take our fingerprints. Needed a comparison. Whatever. I could handle inky fingers, once. That's when it started. Sean spent hours in his room, comparing the prints he found throughout the house on Christmas day against the cards he'd collected with the family prints. Mine, Ted's, the girls, Chantil and Samantha, and of course, his own. He came into the living room with his 'analyses' of the prints later that evening. He discovered both his little sisters had been in his room, and he wasn't very happy about that. Ted's prints were the all over the TV remote. Big surprise. Everyone touched something in the house.

That's when Sean made a startling announcement - one print didn't match anyone in the house. Ted laughed it off, saying it was probably one of the neighbours. I knew I had cleaned the house from top to bottom the day before Christmas, and none of the neighbours had been inside since. The kids had visited friends at their homes, so none of the unidentified prints would be theirs either. Ted insisted that I just missed it when I cleaned. Was that a dig at my housekeeping skills? Sean told me the strange print was found inside on the front doorknob. I made a point of cleaning it, and life went on.

A week later, Sean was at it again. School was back in, and he had printed everyone who dared step inside our house. By now, most of the kid's friends had fingerprint cards in Sean's file box. I drew the line at my friend's and the neighbours. I told him he could only dust the house Saturday mornings, and I would clean in the afternoon. The rest of the week, no fingerprint powder allowed. After having the kit locked up for several days when he used it on a Sunday, he stuck to my rules. His friends had fun with it, but soon became bored. Not Sean. Every weekend out came the power and brush.

Just over a week ago Sean came into the living room with one of his cards. "Hey, Mom," he said. "Found more of those prints again."

He showed me the prints, and I sat down with him and looked at all the cards he'd made. He was right. Those prints didn't belong to anyone in the family, or any of the kid's friends. They did match the other unidentified print he found earlier. There was a really weird pattern in the swirls. More a void than a pattern really. It looked like part of the print was missing. That's about the time I started to freak out, just a little.

I suggested to Ted that we get a security system installed, and he said I was just paranoid. Ta hell with him. I called Alarm Force and got the system installed the next day. I actually felt much better. That weekend we had a small gathering to celebrate Ted's promotion. Naturally Sean came down with his fingerprinting kit. I tried to get him to put it away, but everyone thought it was cute, so, Sean added to his collection, and quickly went to his room to check them out before bedtime.

"Mom," he said next morning. "No one matched that funny fingerprint, or the other one."

Whoa. Other one?

Seems over the weeks Sean found another print that he couldn't match. I wanted to know who the hell was in my house! Nothing was missing. Ted laughed it off again, but it wasn't one of those 'I think you're a little crazy but I love you' laughs. More nervous. I assumed he was just as freaked out as me, but didn't want to say so. Little did I know.

I was more afraid for my kids then anything else. I spent that afternoon going through the house, room by room. Not sure what I was looking for, but I had to look. I checked everything in my room, nothing missing. I was just turning to walk out, when I noticed something. My jewellery box. I'm fussy about where things are, and I knew exactly where on the dresser it should be. It was at least four inches from it's normal spot. I opened it up. Everything had been rearranged, but it was all there. A chill ran down my back. Really. I know a lot of people say that, but it started at the nape of my neck and went straight down my spine. My arms were covered in goose bumps. I felt violated. Now I know why.

This morning, before I headed to work, I triple-checked the alarm. I had to go into the Toronto branch, and was just a block away from the on-ramp to the 404 when the car started acting up. I turned around and drove over to the mechanic's, phoned the office, and got a cab home. Imagine my surprise when I saw Ted's car in the driveway, and a car I didn't recognize parked out front.

I came in, reached to turn the alarm off and noticed it wasn't set. That's when I heard it. I finally understood why Ted was acting weird, why there was no concern about those unidentified prints. He *knew* exactly who they belonged to.

My first thought was *why?* Then I got angry. Something inside me snapped. *How dare he!* I went to the den, unlocked the desk, grabbed the pistol, and loaded it. Your laughter floated down the stairs and filled the house. Time for this this to end.

So, here we are. One totally pissed off woman holding a gun on a naked lady, and I use that word very loosely, sitting on the bed beside my dead husband. I guess you know what's next.

That mattress is going to have to be replaced. It was time for a new one anyway. I'm not sure what I'm going to tell the kids, but I'll think of something.

Nanci M. Pattenden is an author of historical crime fiction, most notably the Detective Hodgins Victorian Mysteries, as well as a professional genealogist.

Cat in a Box

By Jennifer Sharko

Jessica Cline wished she could cry. Her brother Norman, a man with developmental disabilities, was standing on their $10,000 Persian rug and hugging a shabby cardboard box. Jessica stood a metre away from her brother but she could still smell the sweet and unpleasant odour of urine. Inside the box, so she had been told, was a kitten.

"No trouble," Norman whispered as he nodded and shuffled his feet.

Jessica slumped onto the steps leading up to the second floor of their five-bedroom home. Her day couldn't get any worse. That morning Hudson had erupted over the towel colour in the guest bathroom. He raged about hating bright colours. Last month he hated grey tones. At least this time she could hide the bruises.

"You can't keep it, Normy. There's no way Hudson will let you have a cat," she groaned.

"Small cat," Norman whined and pulled the box closer to his chest. The cardboard sides began to collapse under the pressure of his massive hands. "No trouble," he sobbed and clutched the box tighter.

Jessica ripped the box from him grasp and gagged. She was five months pregnant and the stench was intense. She held her breath and gingerly placed the box on the tile floor.

The last thing she needed was a stain on the Persian rug.

Norman sobbed. Jessica rubbed his arm and said, "It's alright Normy. You stopped and the cat's fine."

Five months ago their mother had unexpectedly died and Norman had come to live with them. Hudson had given her six months to find a place for the "retard". He expected a lot of gratitude in return for his kindness.

As Norman sniffled Jessica peered into the shabby container and studied the dark grey creature. It was smaller than she thought it should be. "Where did you get this cat?" she asked.

"Alley," he answered with a hiccup. Norman reached into the box and gently removed the tiny bundle. "Cold," he said and brought the abnormally small feline to his heart. "Hungry," he added and eyed Jessica expectantly. The kitten hadn't reacted to being lifted. It hadn't mewed since coming into the house. Norman brought the animal to his cheek and gently rubbed the soft fur against his skin.

"Maybe you shouldn't do that, Normy. It could be sick," Jessica said and hoped it *was* sick and not dead.

"Doctor!" Norman yelled and wrapped the kitten in the soiled towel from the box. A soft, pitiful mew came from the filthy article. Jessica rubbed her face. Then she realized the vet could explain the situation to Norman and take the blame if the animal needed to be put down.

"That's a great idea. Let's go to that 24-hour animal clinic on Chatsworth Drive," Jessica said and grabbed her jacket from the coat rack. Hudson wouldn't be home for another four hours. They had time to deal with this situation. Norman rocked the cat. Crap, Jessica thought. He was already attached to it.

"Wait, lets use these nicer towels for it," Jessica said. She picked up a blue towel from the pile Hudson had made when he threw them over the second floor railing that morning.

*****

Jessica stretched again. The sterile waiting room chairs were not designed for comfort. Her second trimester was full of nausea, various body aches and anxiety that something was wrong with the baby. She did every early indication test to alleviate her fears. So far there was nothing out of the ordinary, nothing could relieve her stress.

Hudson refused to go to the ultrasounds. He wanted to know it was normal before he'd have anything to do with it. After all, he claimed, she did have "a retard" for a brother which made her a genetic liability. Jessica hated when he called Norman "a retard". She hated herself more for not stopping him.

"Back hurt?" Norman asked. Before Jessica answered his warm knuckles began to kneading her sore spine.

"A little higher, Normy. Perfect," Jessica moaned. The kitten was sleeping, at least she hoped it was sleeping, in Norman's other hand. It fit in his palm. "Looks like you got your hands full," she said and smiled at him.

"Got two hands," he answered and continued the massage until they were called in. Norman held out his hand for Jessica. "Having baby," he told everyone in the waiting room. "Uncle," he added and puffed out his chest. His pride made a few people smile. Others diverted their gaze.

The consultation room had a large stainless steel table in the centre of it. Industrial cleaner had been used on it recently. When Norman gently laid the kitten on the mirrored surface it didn't wake up. Jessica felt its chest to see if it was breathing.

"Hello there. I'm Dr. Nagie," a straight backed woman said as she entered the room. "And who do we have here?"

"Kitten. Cold. Hungry," Norman answered as he gently stroked the tiny creature.

Dr. Nagie studied Norman longer than necessary before she spoke again. "I see. Did you hurt the kitten somehow?" Her voice held a note of anger and condescension.

"Oh no. My brother found the cat in an alley and brought it home. We've had it for less than two hours," Jessica said abruptly.

Dr. Nagie studied Norman again. "How did you find the kitten … ah?"

"Norman," Jessica quickly filled in.

"Norman," the doctor finished.

"Alley. Meow," Norman said emphatically. "Stop meow," he whispered.

"Well, let's take a look." As the vet examined the kitten, Jessica's throat tightened at the thought of explaining the vet bill to Hudson. She couldn't put it on the credit card because he opened the mail. Then she remembered the check book. A wave of relief passed over her when she realized they had Norman's money.

Their mother had asked Jessica to be Norman's legal guardian. She also told Jessica she was leaving her estate to Norman with Jessica and her accountant as the executors. Jessica had agreed to the request without Hudson's knowledge assuming her vibrant mother would live many more decades. Her mother's sudden heart attack at sixty-seven had made the arrangement public.

Hudson demanded the money, but the will was binding. The lawyer explained Jessica could claim a fee for caring for Norman and Hudson reluctantly agreed to the live arrangement. That night he got drunk and demanded sex. The baby was the result.

"Okay, I would say this little fellow is very lucky you came along when you did Norman. But, you may not have realised the kitten has a deformed leg. I have a feeling that's why it was abandoned. Perhaps ..." Dr. Nagie didn't finish the sentence but looked knowingly at Jessica. Jessica watched Norman cuddle the kitten.

"Need love," he whispered. "Food too."

"If we were to keep the ..." Jessica began then stopped abruptly.

"Well, it will need special care and it might be difficult to train," the doctor cautioned.

"I train," Norman hollered. The people in the waiting room must be wondering what was happening.

"We need to think about this. Can you recommend a diet plan?" Jessica asked and swallowed.

*****

Jessica's knuckles turned white on the steering wheel. She blinked back tears and tried to get a grasp on the situation. Hudson would never take in a cat let alone a deformed one. What the hell had come over her. She needed to get rid of it.

"Home?" Norman asked in surprise.

Jessica parked the car. Technically it *was* their home. It was their childhood home. "Why don't we go in and have a look around. Make sure everything's okay," Jessica said. She walked up the familiar pathway and noticed the garden was getting weedy again.

The outdated living room years was full of bittersweet memories. The green walls were covered in an array of frames housing pictures of vacations and holidays, as well as the typical school pictures of her and Norman. A silver frame on the mantle held a picture of her in her wedding gown, alone.

"Miss them," Norman said when Jessica lifted a picture of their dad and mom from a side table.

"Yah, me too Normy," Jessica said and placed the picture carefully back in its spot.

Norman set the kitten on the floor. He got a bowl from the kitchen and gave the kitten some milk. It stumbled and tottered over. "It okay," Norman cooed and scooped the kitten up in his arms. "Normy here." He carefully used a spoon to feed the kitten.

Jessica sank to the floor and Norman joined her. "We'll figure it out somehow," she told him.

Norman said nothing and continued feeding the kitten. His head jerked up. "We live here!" he yelled and pulled Jessica to her feet. He hugged around her expanding waist and danced them back and forth. "Happy again!" he cried.

Jessica started to shake her head but Norman ignored her. "Baby happy! You happy! Tibby happy! Happy," he cried. He let go of her and grabbed the kitten, who must be named Tibby. "Come, Tibby," he crooned as he went down the hallway off the living room to where the bedrooms were located.

Jessica sat down on the couch. The rust coloured piece of furniture was at least thirty years old. Absent mindedly she picked at the short threads of the frayed armrest. The baby kicked inside her and she rubbed the spot soothingly.

She laid her head down on the armrest and wondered if she dared to leave Hudson. That's what Norman meant. She heard Norman showing Tibby around the kitchen. She wished leaving Hudson was as easy as Norman made it seem.

The baby kicked again. Soon this little being would be in the world. Jessica prayed when Hudson saw his child he'd love it as much as she did, but who was she kidding? Tears rolled sideways across her face. This baby would be expected to live up to all the same impossible standards imposed on her.

Norman plopped down on the worn beige carpet with Tibby and another bowl of milk from the clinic. He studied her for a moment. "He not come," Norman said assuredly.

"He'll be angry, Normy," Jessica whispered.

Norman scratched the kitten behind it ears. "We safe here," he answered.

Jessica closed her eyes and tried to figure how to explain why that wasn't true. In her mind she went through various reasons why moving out was impossible.

She didn't' know if it was the safety of the house or Norman's optimism but an escape plan began to form. They had money Hudson couldn't touch. They had a home Hudson could be banned from entering. There was a police file with pictures of bruises. This could work.

Jessica sat up. "Maybe …"

*****

"The retard's in the basement?" Hudson asked. He leaned against the counter as she spooned mashed potatoes onto their plates. It amazed her that she felt no guilt in leaving him. She remembered when she thought he was the most handsome and clever man in the world. Now she saw him as a threat to those she loved.

"Yah, I'm getting him ready to move out. I talked to a case worker today and she said a basement apartment could be ready as soon as the end of the month." Jessica placed the plates on the perfectly set table and lit two candles in crystal holders. Hudson sat at the head of it and she sat on his right.

"And he's going to be eating down there too?" Hudson asked and placed a wedge of steak in his mouth. She hoped it was the way he liked it.

Jessica nodded. If this plan was going to work she had to say very little. But, Hudson was unexpectedly full of questions. Jessica swallowed her steak and continued. "It's best if he gets used to eating by himself."

Hudson nodded and they ate in silence. Then he wiped his mouth and touch Jessica's hand. She froze and waited. "You know he's not so bad if he stays in the basement," he said. "I mean, I know how much you like having your brother around."

Jessica couldn't think. She nodded and went into the kitchen. Was he becoming suspicious? He followed her and her senses heightened. She kept her eyes on the sink filling with sudsy water but listened to his footsteps and his breathing or anything that would give her an early indication that his mood was shifting. He picked up a towel. She thought of what to do if he used it to choke her. Carefully she placed a washed pot on the drying rack.

"I thought you wanted him out," she said evenly. He reached for the pot and dried it. She wondered if it was about to smash into her skull.

"Well, I did or I do, but if he lives and eats in the basement and you take care of him I think I could get used to him being here." Hudson gave her a brilliant smile which turned into a frown when she didn't react quickly enough. "I thought that would make you happy," he said with a menacing undertone.

Jessica's beamed back at him, "Of course it makes me happy. I'm just surprised you changed your mind."

"Aren't I allowed to change my mind." He squeezed her forearm. She knew better then to cry out.

"Absolutely! You're always so thoughtful," she lied and kissed his cheek. His grip didn't ease.

"Good. So no more talk about the retard leaving." He spat the words inches from her face. The flesh of her arm bulged between his fingers. She remained placid until he strolled into the den. When she heard the TV, she exhaled and rubbed her aching limb.

Jessica took a deep breath and then another before she picked up a plate of food and opened the basement door. When Hudson had converted the space to a rec room years ago he hadn't known it served as the perfect hideout for a kitten. The full bathroom housed Tibby's litter box and behind some vodka bottles in the wet bar's fridge were Tibby's milk container.

Norman reached her before she made it to the oak table in front of the TV. He scooped mashed potato into his mouth and devoured all of the white mound in a few forkfuls. With a satisfied smile he rubbed her belly.

"We got a problem," she said and rested her hand on top of his. "Now, Hudson doesn't want you to leave." She planned to use the fake move as a decoy for the real one. It would explain any unexpected phone calls from the accountant or lawyer.

Norman shovelled the steak wedges into his mouth. Jessica scratched the top of the kitten's head. It closed its eyes in pleasure.

"Just leave," Norman said between swallows.

Jessica nodded. "Alright, that's what we'll have to do. But I have to get things organized first and Hudson can't become suspicious. No mistakes, okay? Don't do anything to make him come down here." Jessica stood up. She hadn't felt this empowered or terrified in a long time

"I'll come down after he leaves tomorrow." Jessica kissed her brother on the top of the head and patted Tibby. "Good night you two," she whispered and picked up the dirty dishes.

Hudson hair was visible over the back of the leather couch so Jessica snuck upstairs. As the bathtub filled she examined herself. Fresh bruises were blossoming on her arm. When she went to the accountant tomorrow she would show him the evidence.

They wouldn't be able to stay much longer. She was twenty weeks pregnant and if she wanted to be out of this house and settled before the baby was born she needed to move fast. Hudson's change of opinion should have been expected. Recently when he saw Norman he saw dollar signs. And, a punching bag

*****

Two weeks later Jessica heard the front door slam. She pasted a smile on her face.

"Jessica!" He hollered before he saw her. "Jessica, where the fuck are you?"

She inhaled deeply. The plan was to leave next Friday when Hudson had a late business meeting. As long as his plans didn't fall through they'd move out the second his car turned the corner.

"Hudson, what is it?" she asked steadily and picked up the coat he dumped on the tile floor.

"Did you think I wouldn't find out?" he screamed at her. She stumbled back and hit the wall. He grabbed her arms and shook her hard. "Did you think I wouldn't figure out what you were keeping from me?" Spittle hit her check.

"I don't …" she pleaded.

"Don't lie to me, you worthless bitch! I ran into Ray. He told me about Norman's new pet." Jessica gulped. "He told me about what you were hiding in the basement. Norman was never leaving was he? You lied to me and I hate liars." Hudson let go of her only to punch her in the face. The impact wretched her head back and it hit the wall.

Her vision became fuzzy. She slumped onto the floor and blacked out.

*****

A detective dressed in a cheap suit and a beer gut entered Jessica's hospital room. "Detective Martin," was all he said when Hudson introduced himself and thanked him for coming. Detective Martin sat on the other side of Jessica without being invited to. He stared at the monitors as if he understood the data they produced. Hudson forced himself to remain cool. "I hear the baby will be alright," he said and nodded to the monitor tracking the its heartbeat.

"Yah, the baby's fine," Hudson said and rubbed Jessica's bruised stomach. He'd hoped he gotten rid of it.

Detective Martin took out a note pad. "Can you tell me what happened?" he asked.

"I came home to find my wife on the floor. My brother-in-law was in the basement. I called down to him to ask him what happened. He came up and started throwing punches. He was like an animal. I ran from the house and had a neighbour call 911. You know the rest," Hudson finished. For good measure he picked up Jessica's hand and kissed it. "I don't know what made him snap like that but he needs to be locked up."

Detective Martin wrote down something. Hudson met his stare with cold conviction. He'd no doubt he'd be believed and the retard would be blamed for what happened. He'd be the hero who saved his wife from a freak.

"At the scene you told a police officer you went down to the basement where your brother-in-law lives," Detective Martin stated. His expression and his tone remained even.

Hudson paused then recovered. "That's right, I did go down to the basement. I forgot with everything that's happened," he shrugged. He could handle this idiot.

Detective Martin showed no reaction. "Where did your brother-in-law assault you?" he asked.

Hudson responded confidently. "He hit me once in the basement and then chased me up the stairs when I tried to get away from him."

Detective Martin nodded and looked at the baby's monitor again. "And, who drowned the kitten?"

"Norman," Hudson answered hastily.

"When did he do that?" the detective asked and watched the baby's monitor.

Hudson ran his hands through his hair. Norman had run up the stairs when he heard them fighting. He'd punched Hudson and then shielded Jessica. Norman didn't let go of her even with Hudson beating the shit out of him. Finally, Hudson knocked him out and he collapsed down beside his sister. Then Hudson went into the basement to find the cat. He tossed it into the sink beside the washing machine and filled it with water. He watched the cat try to claw out but eventually the water became too deep. When it stopped moving he went to the neighbour and told him to call 911.

"Maybe Jessica did it," Hudson finally answered.

"Jessica drowned the kitten?" Detective Martin said turning his observant glare back to Hudson.

Hudson ran his hand through his hair again. He liked this story. "It makes sense, doesn't it? Jessica drowned the cat and that set Norman off. He beat her and then attacked me when I got home. The retard needs to be locked up for good." Hudson crossed his arms when he finished and thought some more. "She brought this on herself," he said very pleased with the explanation.

Detective Martin continued to watch him with a level stare. "How would you describe your neighbour, Ray Marshal?"

Hudson was taken aback by the question. "Fine I guess..." Then he realized Ray knew he was angry when he went into the house. "But, he drinks," Hudson continued. "I wouldn't believe much of what he says." Hudson needed to contact Ray immediately to give him the right story. "If you would excuse me for a moment ..."

"Mr. Cline, I need you to come down to the station to make a formal statement. Just so this is sorted out quickly." Detective Martin stood and followed Hudson.

"I want to be here when Jessica wakes up," Hudson responded stopping on the threshold of the hospital room.

"Yes, I'm sure you do," Detective Martin agreed and smiled slightly. It was the first emotion the man had exhibited. "I have a colleague who will remain with your wife. We will inform you when she wakes up."

"But, I have to be here ... to support her," Hudson said and stepped closer to him. Detective Martin's eyes narrowed and Hudson backed down. Instead he walked back to the chair he vacated earlier. "I won't leave her side and I know my rights." His eyes meet the detective's and dared him to contradict him.

"Fine, then we can wait together," Detective Martin said and sat across from Hudson.

Jessica stirred. Hudson's clenched his jaw. Detective Martin smiled again.

Jennifer Sharko worked for over a decade as an art psychotherapist in the palliative care field, and with developmentally delayed individuals. After the birth of her second daughter in 2010 she became a stay-at-home-parent and learned to crochet, run, and write.

The Handbag Whisperer

By Harry Posner

M arlee's was a popular destination in Midvale, especially on a hot summer's day like this one. Practically everyone in town had the same thought at the same time: "Hey, let's go for an ice cream." And so the line-up snaked its way from the garage-sized hut past the fire engine red picnic tables, almost reaching the edge of the parking lot.

It was like one of those hot summer days when, as a child, Doris would walk with her family to the local ice cream parlor, come away with cones of Maple Walnut, Rocky Raccoon, Pistachio Party, Cherry Swirl. She and her two sisters would sit in the park beside the creek, licking away in total silence. Although they didn't know it at the time, eating an ice cream cone is a kind of meditation, requiring both focus and efficiency. But more than that, it is also a moment of pure, unadulterated bliss, and the one memory of childhood that Doris had always treasured.

She had arrived at Marlee's just as the sun was at its peak, driving people towards the cool delights of Raspberry Rose and Strawberry Ripple, Caramel Carnival and Espresso Dream. Doris was near the front of the line and had to make that always difficult decision: Double Dutch Chocolate or Orange Sherbet. She wiped away the beads of sweat on her forehead and weighed the two cones in her mind. Creamy cocoa coolness versus sweet tart sharpness. Classic chocolate versus upbeat orange. What did she feel like? How *was* she feeling, exactly, on this rather special day, the 1st anniversary of her late husband's death? Overweight, undesirable, a cloud of sadness inside her heart.

She stood in line at Marlee's Ice Cream Shop, thinking about Don and their years together. They produced just the right number of children, raised them as well as can be expected, and sent them out into the world. But was she ever truly happy? Did she choose the right man? God, how she missed him. And who was she, now that he was gone? *A lonely old woman past your prime*, she said to herself, and once again imagined reaching for the container of sleeping pills sitting on her nightstand. She would have broken down into tears had she not been in public, standing in line at Marlee's, having to make a decision. Doris gazed back up at the selection board, but what she saw sent an electric shock shivering through her body. For the flavor names on the board had disappeared, replaced by strange and dark interlopers:

> Attraction's Absence
> Nutty Melancholy
> Quotidian Drudge
> Desire's Demise
> Anger's Appetite
> Regretful Swirl
> Ridiculous Hope

Bitterness Blast

Resignation Ripple

Doris approached the window, her mouth half open, eyebrows knitted.

"What can I get ya?" said the red-haired girl from behind the counter.

"Oh, uh, I'd like a small cone of..." Doris looked back up at the board, but it hadn't changed.

"Uh, ... the other flavors, are they still available?"

"Just what's on the board, ma'am."

Crazy thoughts raced through her head: Alzheimer's. Heat Stroke. Psychotic Breakdown. What the hell was happening? The folks farther back in the line began to grumble.

"Can we hurry this up, please?"

"Today, some time, would be good."

Doris had to choose, and she had to do it now. "Ridiculous Hope," she blurted.

The girl shouted to the back, "One small Ridic!" She turned to Doris. "$3.50, ma'am."

Doris reached into her oversized handbag, her fingers fumbling their way past a wad of tissues, her compact, a pair of gloves, sunglasses, a lotto ticket, grocery receipts, a bag of cat treats, six elastics, make-up kit, lip balm, tweezers, tiger head key fob, travel size deodorant stick, a dog-eared copy of *To Kill a Mockingbird*, two packs of chewing gum, an unpaid hydro bill, and a cashless wallet, searching for three dollars and fifty cents in change hiding somewhere at the bottom of a bottomless pit. She became more agitated by the second, as the people in line, sweating in the relentless heat, began to lose it:

"There ought to be a law!"

"What the hell's wrong with you, lady?"

"Hurry the goddamn up!"

Just as Doris was about to give up and turn away from the window, a gentle voice from behind wafted over her shoulder. "Looks like you need a hand." A tall man, perhaps in his early fifties, with salt and pepper hair and moist grey eyes set into a kind face, stood there smiling. He pulled out a business card and offered it to her. On the card was printed:

JON ZAFTIG

HANDBAG WHISPERER

Because sometimes we can't find it alone

"May I?" he asked, nodding toward her handbag. Doris, caught completely off guard, just blinked. "Help. May I help?" he added.

Without thinking, Doris handed him her bag. What possessed her to give her purse to a total stranger, she'll never know. The man took it from her, raised it up to his face, opened it, and reached in, his cheek resting against the brown leather surface like he was doing a slow dance with it. As he rooted about, his eyes gazed into Doris', as if to say, "Remember that as long as there is kindness in the world, hope stands a chance." And he was smiling all the time, like he knew that it would all turn out fine, that she'd one day find her way back to that moment of childhood bliss in the park. That, at the bottom of every life, there remain a few extra coins of possibility, waiting patiently for the right pair of fingers to snatch them up.

"Here we are," said the man, as he pulled out exactly three dollars and fifty cents in change, and handed it to her. Without another word he passed her the handbag, turned and walked away.

"Here you go," said the red-haired girl behind the counter, as she extended the ice cream cone.

"Thank you," said Doris, her voice trembling. She took the cone in hand, orange sherbet already beginning to melt its way over the top edge of the crisp shell. She decided to walk to the park, cone in one hand, the man's card in the other. She reached the park and found a quiet spot near the creek, the perfect place to meditate on the sweet tart sharpness of life. To eat her cone in silence, focused and efficient, and, thanks to the handbag whisperer, now connected to something called ridiculous hope.

A member of Words Aloud poetry collective, the Headwaters Writers Guild, Writers Ink Alton, and Associate Member of the League of Canadian Poets, **Harry Posner** has published books of poetry--*Wordbirds*; novels--*Charivari* and *A Softness in the Eyes*; flash fiction--*Little Exits*; and a CD of audio poetry--*In The Event of True Happiness*.　　www.posnerbooks.com

Stanley

By Sylvia DeLisa

I glanced out the window. Carolina, my neighbour, was struggling to shovel snow from the pathway leading to her front door. Recently, she'd retired as a principal at a Catholic elementary school. I worried about her. She was not only my neighbour but also my dearest friend. I opened the door and called out to her to come over for coffee and a chat. She waved and said she would be over as soon as she finished.

I went into the kitchen to make the coffee and pondered her situation. She spoiled her husband Stanley, made sure his meals were always on time, and looked after her three daughters. Although they were away in university, Carolina did everything for them.

"Hello," Carolina shouted as she came into the house. I hugged her and took off her coat. She sat down, I poured her a coffee, and placed a plate of cookies and brownies on the table. We talked about what we did during the week and caught up on some of the neighbourhood gossip. Then Carolina confessed that there was a three-month teaching position available in the southern part of Africa. The teacher she would replace was quite ill and they needed a substitute. She'd never been to Africa and she really wanted to go.

"What about Stanley, what does he think about all this?" I asked.

"I haven't discussed it with him yet. But the more I talk about it the more I want to go."

"I understand," I said, and told her if she did, I would be more than willing to give Stanley his meals and help him in anyway possible.

"I'll pay you," Carolina said.

I shook my head. "No, I want to do this for you. You've been good to me in the past and helped me when my husband passed away."

We spent the rest of the afternoon making arrangements and were quite excited about her trip. When she left I watched her cross the street. Well, well Stanley, I thought, Carolina might take your nonsense but I won't.

Three days later Carolina phoned me to confirm her date of departure. I cleared my calendar of all my activities for the next three months then called my family and friends to tell them what I would be doing.

On the Saturday after Carolina left, I called Stanley to ask how he was coping. He was upset. I listened to him rant about Carolina leaving him.

"I'll be over tomorrow to make your dinner," I said. That wasn't good enough for him. No one except Carolina should be cooking for him. Carolina had told me that if she was late with one of his meals or he found a wrinkle on a shirt there was hell to pay.

He never lifted a finger to help her. She did the gardening, paid the bills and looked after the household while Stanley watched television. I decided if he gave me any trouble while she was away I would let him have a piece of my mind. At six o'clock the next day I took him his dinner along with a few frozen lunches that he could microwave.

Stanley opened the door. He smiled and hugged me. I was astounded. Who was this man? He wasn't miserable at all. In fact, he was nice. So I stayed and kept him company while he ate.

He raved about my cooking and kept smiling and winking at me. During dessert he reached over and squeezed my thigh. *Oh Boy, what have I gotten myself into.* I knew I was an attractive woman, at least for a woman in her early fifties, but since my husband died I wasn't interested in getting involved with anyone, especially Stanley.

The days went by, I took over his meals and attended to the chores at their house. I enjoyed the talks that Stanley and I had. I'd always thought he was a stupid man, but he surprised me. He knew a lot about politics, books and music.

One night he kissed me. I was shocked. My best friend was in Africa and her husband was hitting on me. I wasn't having any of it. Over the weeks he kept telling me how lonely he was and pressing me to have sex with him. I didn't want to cheat with my friend's husband but he wore me down and I relented.

"This is the only time Stanley," I said. Of course that didn't happen and it turned into a full-blown affair.

What else can I say, except that he soon turned from being nice to being belligerent. If I said no, he forced himself on me. I grew to detest him and started to think of ways to get rid of him. If Carolina went through this she would thank me. So I ground up all of my sleeping pills and slipped into his beer.

The next day I found him lying on the floor. I tried to move him but he was too heavy. I dialed 911. An ambulance and the police arrived. They pronounced him dead. I started to cry, not really, they were more crocodile tears. The police patted me on my shoulder and said they were sorry about my husband.

Two days later when Carolina came home, I told her the whole story. I thought she would have been glad that I got rid of Stanley for her.

No.

My trial is pending.

At 77 years old, Sylvia DeLisa is a newcomer to the writing world. Except for her short story, Stanley, she uses her own life experiences in her stories. Along with writing fiction, she is working on her memoir for her children and grandchildren.

Only Jacob
By Sheila Horne

Jacob showed up at Mrs. Labelle's rooming house the summer I started reading *Wuthering Heights*. Papa wasn't happy about me reading what he called a grown up book. He complained to Mama that I shouldn't fill my twelve-year-old head with such nonsense. I should stick to the *Nancy Drew*, and *Hardy Boy* books I ran to get at the library every Saturday afternoon.

"Papa, leave her books alone," mama said. "She's old enough and a good reader, you should be proud." Then she coughed and slammed the bedroom door.

I listened to them discussing my reading as I sat in the shade of our concrete porch watching Jacob. He spent most of his time across the street in Trinity Bellwoods Park fighting demons he felt made the park and street unsafe. To us living on Trinity Avenue, Jacob with his tangled hair, rotting Yankees baseball cap, dirty clothes, and worn out shoes, was harmless. To passengers squeezed tight in streetcars and pedestrians walking through the park and on Queen Street, he was a filthy lunatic. I thought Jacob a prince from a far off land left to forage for the rest of his life. On his good days, he pitched ball for the boys playing baseball in the park. He told them stories about when he was a boy, and his father took him to Yankee Stadium to see the Yankees play. He was the best road hockey goalie, the boys ever had, and he happily turned rope for us girls skipping on the sidewalk.

On his bad days, Jacob ripped up floorboards and punched holes in the walls of Mrs. Labelle's house searching for a mythical creature, he said pried his eyes open at night, and dug little sharp claws into his legs while he slept. On those days he also threw garbage cans around the street, and chased cars while barking like a dog.

"It's only Jacob," I would yell to papa when he asked about the commotion. Then either papa or someone else on the street would phone the police.

"I apologize for the uproar," Jacob always said as he waved his handcuffed wrists and slid into the back of the yellow police cruiser.

Everyone on the street knew Constable Fields. Papa often gave him a glass of water. He'd gulp the water, then lightly slap papa on his back and shake his head as papa bent down to look at Jacob sitting in the car.

"Jacob," papa would say, "get better and come back quick." Straightening up he'd shake his finger at Constable Fields and tap the top of the car letting him know it was okay to leave.

Jacob always returned a few weeks later, quieter and distant. He slept all day on the parched grass under a blistering summer sun.

Every day papa drove off in his old black Chevrolet truck with the muffler held up with a piece of wire. He returned with broken console televisions, vacuum cleaners, and other appliances. I held the door open as he hauled them down to his repair shop in the basement of our house while mama watched from her seat at the kitchen table.

"Is good Louisa," papa often said to her, "I am my own boss, I can look after you and Freida."

Mama would nod, then cough, and spit into the handkerchief she carried, then fold it and shove it back into the pocket of her orange floral housecoat.

Papa took over the running of the house. He gave me fifty cents on Saturdays for helping with the chores. I quickly spent the money at Mr. Kovel's Tobacco and Gift Store on *16* and *Tiger Beat* magazines. Papa disliked wasting money on what he called stupidity. So I sat on the store's dusty wooden floor and flipped through the magazine pages then stuck them under my shirt, and snuck them into my room. Once, after I had finished reading a *Photo Play* magazine with Elizabeth Taylor on the cover, I left it for Jacob under his tree in the park. Later, I saw him lying on the bench. He had the magazine over his face, and the picture of Elizabeth Taylor pinned to his shirt.

Papa also supervised mama's garden. "We want them nice for mama Frieda," he'd say as I watered her plants.

The truth was, mama no longer cared about the flowers she had once planted. She no longer enjoyed her garden or came out of the house. She spent her days and nights shut away in her room. The closed wooden shades and door not only kept the sunlight and noise out, they kept me out. When she did venture onto the porch, she sat with her arms wrapped tightly around her body, rocking back and forth, watching Jacob.

"What you looking at mama?" I asked her one day. I needed her to smile at me. I needed her to mess up my hair, kiss me on top of my head, and call me her beloved and most favourite person in the world, like she had in past years. Instead, she turned, gazed at me for a moment, and ran her fingers across my cheek.

"Only Jacob," she rasped. For an instant I thought I saw half a smile cross her face before she coughed, and headed into the house.

With Jacob living on our street, a police car in front of Mrs. Labelle's rooming house soon became normal. But it was an ambulance on the street one evening that brought the neighbours out to stand on the sidewalk. Robbie, the boy who lived three doors down, fell off his bike in the park, and hit his head on the gravel pathway. Everyone watched as the ambulance drove away with Robbie and his hysterical mother. Robbie's father maneuvered his green Chevy Nova through the idle crowd and followed the ambulance. Eventually, the neighbours returned to the coolness of their houses, thanking the Lord it was not their crisis. Papa, Jacob and I stood in the park. Tears had washed a trail of grime down Jacob's face and neck. It ended at the collar of his shirt.

"I'm sorry," he sobbed, "I'm sorry. I couldn't save him … they're too fast."

Papa gently led him into our house. "It's okay, Jacob, all will be fine, the evil ones they gone now." He spoke to him, the same way I heard him quiet mama late at night.

Before he entered our house, Jacob took off his cap. He licked his hand, smoothed his sweaty hair and adjusted his collar. I knew then, that Jacob, like Heathcliffe, had lost a great love, perhaps named Cathy, and had run away from a grand life to save us.

"Who's there?" Mama yelled.

"It's only Jacob, mama," I said, running into the hallway.

She stood at the top of the stairs. I thought she would come down, and make lemonade like she used to do when company came to visit. She didn't. She went back to her room and I returned to the kitchen. Jacob and papa sat at our table, glasses of coke in front of them. Papa's hand seemed large around the crystal glass. Jacob eyed his glass. Then he picked it up, took a sip, put the glass back on the table and left. I ran down the hall after him. I wanted to ask him to keep the demons away from us, the ones that threatened to take my mother. He could do it. I knew he could. After all he was the protector of the street, the park and everything good. But before I reached the front door, it closed and he was gone. I went back into the kitchen, and turned on the tap.

Then winter came, cold and snowy. The only footprints in the silent white park belonged to Jacob. They looked as though he'd run crisscross around the park and played hopscotch in the snow. One day they stopped.

"Moved on," Mrs. Labelle said, sweeping the snow away from her walkway. "Kensington Market sounded like a good idea to him."

I thought of Jacob often. Especially the following summer while I sat with papa and the neighbours on chairs lined up against the wall in our stifling living room. Jacob had cried for Robbie the year before, and he would cry for mama now. No one in the airless room cried. The women just sat with their fat black-stocking legs crossed at the ankles, fanning themselves with unused starched handkerchiefs. Their skinny husbands tugged at the necks of their stiff white shirts and drank papa's vodka. Papa looked uncomfortable. If he wanted to cry, it didn't show.

"She's in good place," Mrs. DaSilva said, patting me on the hand. "Is happy now."

Mrs. Peireira nodded. "She is right. No more suffering. Poor little Louisa, all that she suffered."

"Your papa, he knows the suffering, he knows is best," Mrs. DaSilva added.

They went on to say God had magnificent plans for my mama, an angel on earth now one of God's angels in heaven.

"Ungrateful to shed tears," Mrs. Rodrigues said. She made the sign of the cross. They all made the sign of the cross.

At that moment, I jumped up. I ran out the front door

and down the street. I ran past Mr. Kovel's shop. I ran past the bank. I ran past the cheese shop, the bakery, and old men picking their teeth outside stores with fruit and vegetables rotting in the heat. I ran down Augusta Avenue, past brightly painted houses with statues of Mary, and Jesus on small manicured lawns. I had prayed to them, including the angels and all the saints, but no one answered. I ran past mothers walking babies, and children skipping rope, and old women sweeping sidewalks, and tricycles, and bicycles, and cars, and vans, and trucks honking their horns. I ran to Kensington Market.

Previously published in CommuterLit, April 2012

Sheila Horne's articles, poems and short stories have been published in various magazines and anthologies. She facilitates writing programs and is a member of The Markham Village Writers and The Writers' Community of York Region.

Dove's Sacrifice ~ *a true story*

By MJ Moores

E very nerve ending in my body vibrated as I stood outside that hospital room. My hands shook as I finally accepted a tissue from the nurse.

"Are you ready to go in?"

I shook my head *no*, even as I clawed back the sob threatening to vault from my lips. Pushing hot tears from my face with the back of one hand, I blew my nose with the other.

Trying to force deep breaths into tight lungs, my body wrung them out of me again. I stared, but I didn't, at the contrast of the nurse's dark skin where it met her blue scrubs. My usually ordered thoughts no better than flashing yellow lights in a storm.

The memory of the tremor of my mother's voice brought me back to our phone conversation yesterday…

"I have some bad news," I said.

Mom's breath became shallow and distant. Static clouded the line. I envisioned her holding the phone to her chest.

"What is it?" She asked, more wary than usual.

"Dad's dying."

"No…" the word wavered. Even though they separated thirty-five years before, she still loved the man – or at least the man he once was.

She'd hit a black bird three days earlier. An omen her Cree friend told her meant the impending death of a loved one. I'm not particularly spiritual, but this unsettled me.

I'd only found out about Dad the morning of that call. I was told he had two months to live. Hearing he was dying felt like the finale to a slow-motion recoil from a pistol shot. After a scare seven years ago we all knew it was going to hit, we just didn't know when. Back then he'd chosen to ignore the doctor's warning in favour of living his life, his way. Shortly after that, he broke his sobriety and I broke with him.

After hanging up with Mom, reality slammed back into place. I had to call my half-brother James, also estranged from our father. Those two were so much alike they couldn't stand each other on principal. Though James had grown up apart from Dad, the two were clearly hewn from the same cloth. We'd agreed to visit Dad in *one week*, that would give me enough time to get a referral to see a counsellor and get my head on straight. I couldn't walk into that hospital room before then.

I knew I could say 'good-bye.' The idea of my father being absent from my life was nothing new. What I *couldn't* do was say 'hello' – not without the ice crystallizing my blood, then the anger alternately melting and boiling it again.

The next day I took my son to pre-school, went grocery shopping, and only thought about my father enough to make plans to call for that appointment. I had the necessary time to deal with this news and I wasn't about to let him dictate my actions. But driving home that afternoon, along a barren country road, something inexplicable happened.

A mourning dove flew down and landed on the road ahead. It flutter-hopped and settled to peck at something in my lane.

Whatever, I thought.

It'll move in a minute.

It didn't.

Too used to humans, I guess. It'll take off in a second.

I took my foot off the accelerator and frowned.

IT'S NOT MOVING!

Thwunk.

"What was that Mommy?"

I looked in the rear-view mirror... that poor, stupid bird waited until the car drove over top of it to fly away. It writhed, helpless, one wing opened to the sky in the midst of that desolate road. My chest constricted. My lungs tightened. The burn of it branded the image of that struggling bird on my already confused mind.

I bit my lip, then said, "Nothing, Sweetie. Just a rock."

I decided *not* to go home. Instead, I took my son to the bookstore where he could play with the train set and I could lose myself in another world.

Seven hours after killing that bird, I arrived home to a single message on my answering machine.

I returned the call.

"What's going on?" I asked my step-mother, Helen.

"Your dad's in too much pain. He's denied treatment and switched to palliative care."

"What does that mean?"

"They don't think he'll make it through the night."

A wad of fear vaulted from my heart into my throat.

I coughed.

"I'll be right there."

I took nothing with me, not a kiss from my husband or a hug from my son. I got in the car and drove. Terror plummeted to the pit of my stomach with every inhalation, only to inch its way back up on the exhale. With every jolting breath in, I scolded myself for driving alone. On every upward thrust of air bolts of anger and grief struck out.

What if he says something snide when I walk in?

It's about time.

I pushed that one aside.

'Hi Dad, long time.' Then I'll give him a hug.

What the hell are you doing here?

That would never work.

Hey, old man... didn't think you'd get out of seeing me again, did you?

Nothing's changed.

Tears welled-up but I'd smash them back down again. The rollercoaster ride had my body vibrating – numb one minute, electric the next.

I pulled into the hospital parking lot, turned off the car, and gripped the steering wheel forcing deep, even breaths into my body.

The shaking stopped.

I got out and followed the directions to his room. Along the halls a dozen or more photocopied signs told me exactly what to do: go to the nurse's desk, register, then go to the room. I latched onto and repeated those simple steps over and over, the rigid normalcy of it a balm to my frayed nerves.

A nurse sat at the station writing on a chart, her head lowered. I'd seen enough TV to know better than to disturb her. An older gentleman also stood waiting. I leaned on the tall desk.

The nurse startled and looked at me.

"He was here first," I said.

She smiled. "He's always here. What can I do for you?"

"I'm here to register."

"Excuse me?"

"To sign in."

"You don't need to –"

I grabbed the 8 ½ x 11 sheet of paper posted with a single strip of scotch-tape and shook it at her.

"These signs say *new visitors have to check in*. I'm doing what it – My father is dying!"

Gobs of salty tears broke free. I gripped the counter to keep from falling as my body shook, fracturing my attempts to rebuild control. She came around the desk and held a tissue box out. I ignored it. Instead, she walked me down the hall, guiding me in a way better suited to that old man.

Standing with me outside room 2428, she was a pillar of stability and compassion. Her simple presence allowed me to mentally latch onto her, even as I stood tall fighting the tears. For ten minutes I breathed deeply, first replaying the mockery of events in the past twenty-four hours, and then shoring up walls, plastering over time-worn cracks. I thought I had more time.

I nodded to the nurse and said, "Okay."

As she led me across that threshold, my walk morphed to a stride as I left the blubbering mess of myself behind.

"Hey old man... didn't think you'd get out of seeing me again did you?"

Helen stood up, hugged me and then left with the nurse.

Dad looked at me.

Hopped up on morphine, he felt no pain. The man who somewhat resembled the father I knew seven years ago smiled back at me and laughed like a child.

The drugs dissolved his anger and my fear.

I sat down in the vacated chair.

I wasn't looking for the words I knew he'd never say. But because of another of his selfish decisions I wouldn't even get to hear him say *I missed you*.

I held his large, imposing hand. A hand that had shied away from mine at my mother-in-law's funeral. A hand that had never known the strength of a daughter's grip or the feel of the tenacity with which she tried to prove herself.

Though I stayed the entire night to support Helen, it wasn't until three days after the morning I left his bed-side that I got *the call*. He'd finally passed on June 24th, four days before his birthday on the 28th: 24 – 28 …

A week later a friend of mine looked up the meaning of *mourning doves*, when I'd explained the strange happening and bizarre numerical coincidences – told me the birds were more a sign of peace than death.

I didn't want that dove's sacrifice to have been in vain. I knew that one day I might be able to forgive my father, forgive myself even … but *the road is long with many a winding turn*.

A university graduate of Theatre Production with a minor in creative writing and a BEd, MJ cannot help but combine her passions for the makebelieve and bring them to life both on the page and on the stage. http://mjmoors.com

www.infinite-pathways.org

www.ingramcontent.com/pod-product-compliance
Lightning Source LLC
Chambersburg PA
CBHW060816120626
46557CB00001B/236